Shattered ILLUSION

LISAMARIE KADE

COPYRIGHT

Shattered Illusion
The Red Society
Book One

Copyright © 2022 by Lisamarie Kade

Kade Publishing LLC

Cover Design by Amanda Walker PA & Design Services

Edited and proofreading by Magnolia Author Services

This book is a work of fiction. Names, characters, places, and incidents either are products of the author's imagination or are used fictitiously. Any resemblance to actual events, locals, or persons, living or dead is coincidental.

All rights reserved.

No part of this book may be reproduced in any form or by any electronic or mechanical means, including information storage and retrieval systems, without written permission from the author, except for the use of brief quotations in a book review.

❀ Created with Vellum

NOTE TO READERS:

This book contains topics that may be sensitive to some.

*Past childhood trauma /abuse
*Mentions of domestic abuse / assault
While the story does not go into specific detail of abuse, it is
still mentioned.

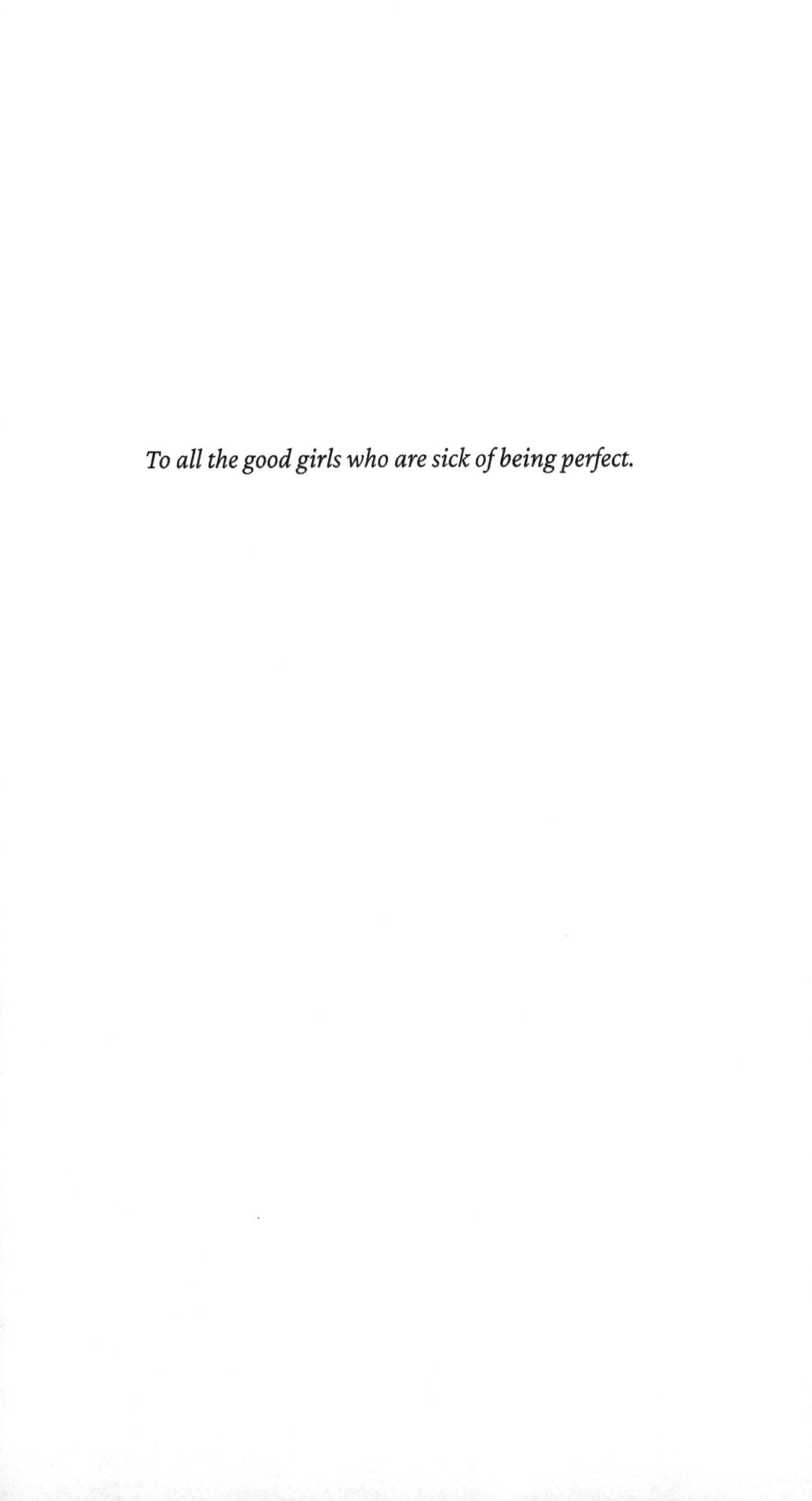

To all the good girls who are sick of being perfect.

1

CHARLA

My name is Charla Krauss, and this is my story.

"Come on, Char... It will be fun. You'll get to enjoy a few drinks and watch me act a fool."

I smile a little at the thought of my best friend drunk at a high-end strip club. Then I groan because it's really not my idea of a good time.

"Can't we just go to beach side and have a few drinks, eat caviar?"

"No, that's not what I want to do to celebrate my twenty-eight years on this Earth."

I sigh. "Fine, Spencer, but you owe me for this."

Spencer claps his hands together once and winks at me before heading out of my office. Thank God because now I can focus on this project and not be distracted by all the craziness he brings when he enters a room.

An hour later the task I was working on is complete. That leaves my agenda open for the remainder of the day. I page Spencer's office to see about leaving early. I wouldn't mind hitting the spa on the way home. A hot stone massage sounds perfect right about now.

"Yes, beautiful?"

"Will it be all right if I head out for the day? The Booker account has been all set up and I already emailed it to you."

"That's fine. I'll see you tomorrow, yeah?"

"Yes, sir."

That's one of the perks of working under your best friend. He rarely tells me no. We end the call and I start to gather up my belongings when my phone dings.

```
     Dinner at 6:30 sharp, don't be late.
```

So much for my massage. I have to mentally remind myself not to rub my hands down my face in annoyance. My makeup can't be messed up. It's perfect. Just like it is every day. It must remain perfect.

```
       Yes, Father, see you soon.
```

Considering he didn't list a restaurant, I know dinner will be at the Krauss family home.

```
Corey will be there too, so I expect you to
          act like a lady this time.
```

Fuck me. I don't want to have dinner with Corey. Not now, not ever. I don't know why my father insists on putting us in the same room. Wait, yes, I do. My father demands I marry into money, and money Corey has. He is also a pig. A womanizer, if you will. I don't want anything to do with him. He is into politics just like my father and so that qualifies him as the perfect candidate.

Ha.

I will admit the man is hot. Corey is probably six-two, with perfectly styled blonde hair. His brown eyes have a twinkle to them that have the chicks dropping their panties left and right. He has a nice body. No complaints there. Wait, yes, I have complaints. He doesn't wow me in bed. Yup, I was dumb enough to sleep with the man a time or two.

My father introduced the two of us about a year or so ago. He was charming, said all the right words. I fell for that charm and the minute he got me in bed, all bets were off. He only cared about his own desires, his own pleasure. He was arrogant about it too. Let me tell you, it was a turn-off. Soon after, I started to see Corey differently, less attractive, but after a gala and one too many glasses of champagne, I ended up in his bed. It was just as bad as the first time and sobered me right up. From that moment on, I learned to never drink when Corey was present.

As I climb into my silver Lexus SUV, aka Sexy Beast, I silently curse my father for being the way he is. His outrageous demands wear me down. I have tried to explain numerous times my feelings about Corey, yet Daddy refuses to hear it.

It doesn't take me long to reach my father's house, I

mean mansion. It's tucked away in a gated community with other lavish homes full of wealthy people. Their well-manicured lawns complete the perfect look. But I know, not everything you see is as good as it looks.

Walking up to the door, I think back to the last time Corey was over. My father kept making snide remarks about the two of us and how we would be perfect for each other. I smiled through most of it, trying my best to just let it go. After all, Daddy just wants what is best for his princess. However, the minute Corey cornered me when I came out of the bathroom, I grew pissed.

Corey tried to kiss me. I refused, pushing away from him. He didn't like that one bit, he told me when I became his, he would make sure I was an obedient woman.

I lost my shit. Daddy was not happy about it either, in fact, he apologized to Corey for my outburst, which caused me to storm out and not speak to my father for over a week.

Now here I am about to bite my tongue until it is sure to bleed, just to appease my father.

Once I ring the bell, one of the housekeepers opens it immediately. I smile warmly and walk in. I already know everyone will be gathered in the sitting room, so I stop at the guest bathroom to freshen up and delay showing my beautiful face, as my father tells me often.

I shouldn't complain about the way my father is. He raised me on his own for about eight years before my stepmother came along. Daddy put me in the best private schools in the area, and he kept me on a tight leash, making sure I grew up to be the perfect daughter. One who wouldn't tarnish his image, once he told me that he raised me the way he did because he didn't want me to turn out like my mother. I've never met the woman and, based on the stories I've been told, I'm glad. I'm grateful for my daddy, it's just sometimes his actions piss me off. There's a knock at the door, bringing me from my thoughts. I open it to see Corey standing there looking smug. Asshole.

"Charla, I thought I heard you come in."

"I did."

I watch as his eyes take me in from head to toe. I don't miss it when they pause at my breasts. It makes me feel gross. My cream v-neck blouse is hardly sexy, however, it's clear that Corey likes what he sees. It makes me cringe internally.

"Was there something you needed, Corey?"

"Just admiring the goods." He winks.

Such a pig. I roll my eyes and make a move to walk past him, but he grabs my wrists, halting me.

"I think I deserve a kiss from my future wife, what do you say?"

"Corey, I will never be your wife." I yank my wrist free and brush past him, calling for my father as I go. "Father?"

Quickly walking, I make it to the sitting room before Corey can harass me further. I see everyone has drinks in their hands. Great.

"Charla, dear, I thought I heard you." My father sounds sincere but based on the amber liquid in the tumbler his holding, he is anything but. He places a quick kiss on my cheek.

"Father." My tone is clipped. "If you insist on putting Corey and I in the same room, you need to remind him to mind himself. I am not his possession."

"Charla," my father warns, but I don't care.

"Don't Charla me. I will not be spoken to in such a manner that Corey feels is acceptable. Cornering me in the bathroom, yet again, and demanding things from me will not be tolerated."

Daddy's eyes go wide.

I can't tell if I've embarrassed him or if he is outraged. Sometimes it is hard to read him. I've been conditioned to fall in line and do what is expected. It gets old, even now that I'm a grown woman. He scares me, however, tonight I draw the line.

My father reaches for my elbow, gripping it firmly as he guides me to a quiet corner. Surely to reprimand me like a child.

"What has gotten into you? I expect better from you."

Of course, he does. He always does.

"I expect better of your company. I am not some prized trophy to be won."

"Excuse me?" Daddy's eyes nearly pop out of his head.

"I said, I expect better of your—"

"I heard you, Charla. Why can't you just get along with Corey? I'm trying to secure your future."

"See, Daddy, that's where you are wrong. I don't need you to secure anything for me. I can find a man on my own."

"I know you can, but I want you to be with someone worthy."

I laugh. "I can assure you; Corey is not and will never be worthy of me."

I reach out and pat my father's chest before walking away.

I win this round.

2

CHARLA

I don't know how I allowed Spencer to talk me into his shenanigans. Here I sit at a strip club, and not just any strip club. It's a club downtown that only caters to the wealthy and possibly the famous who frequent this city. Jacksonville is full of both, though right now with a glance around the place, I'd say it is mostly filled with old rich men who only have one thing on their mind.

Gross.

I smile as the waitress comes up to take our drink order. She's dressed in a see-through body suit that has just a little lace flower pattern over her nipple. She's wearing fishnets under the thong suit and nothing else except a pair of sky-high pink heels.

How can she enjoy working in this environment?

"What can I get for you this evening, miss?" The waitress smiles and it seems genuine, which shocks me a little.

"I'll have a martini, please."

She looks from me to Spencer. "And for you, sir?"

I smile and continue taking her in. She has short black

hair and her eyes are dark. I bet she's pretty when she's not here.

"I'll take a rum and coke, top-shelf rum," Spencer's stern voice tells the waitress.

"I'll be right back." She smiles and walks off, shaking her ass. It makes me want to roll my eyes.

"I'd hit that."

"I know you would, ass."

Spencer has always been cocky, even as a kid. I got used to it and didn't take his shit. It's probably why we are the best of friends now. Over time, I have found a few soft spots in him; he doesn't let them show as often as I would like, but that's Spencer for you.

"So, how long do I need to stay before I can leave without you pitching a fit?"

"Not anytime soon, Charla. The night is young and we are celebrating!"

"Great," I moan, throwing my head back. I really don't want to be in this club. It's not my scene. I'm too good for this place.

"Oh, come on, it's not that bad. Maybe we can find you a single guy for the night. You need to get laid."

"Excuse me? I do not. I'm doing just fine, thank you." It's a lie, one he will see right through. Truth be told, it has been a while. I won't admit that to him though.

"Your trusty vibe ain't got a tongue though."

I gasp.

"Here are your drinks."

I turn quickly, I didn't realize the waitress was back with our drinks. I'm hoping like hell she didn't hear Spencer's crude words. I watch as she hands him his drink and then hands me mine.

"Can I get you two anything else?"

"No, I think we are good for now, thanks."

The waitress nods and leans down to my ear. "It's okay, babe, vibrators are more trustworthy than a man." She winks at me as she turns and goes.

"Holy shit, Char, you are turning red. Did I embarrass you?" Spencer bursts out laughing.

"Thanks for that, asshole."

"Anytime."

I take a sip of my drink and say nothing more as I glance around this place. There's no way I would let these men who are most likely my daddy's age or older touch me. I would consider sleeping with Corey before any of them and that says a lot. Ugh. Vibrator it will be tonight.

Spencer sets his tumbler down hard. "Time for another." He stands and walks off to the bar, leaving me.

When he arrives back, I notice he is distracted and staring at the stage. He is totally checking the stripper out. Blonde hair cascades down over her shoulders as she grinds against the pole.

"Earth to Spence,"

"Yeah, sorry."

"I see you." I laugh, he hates being caught. I glance back at the dancer who is now topless. How do women feel okay with this? Does that make me a prude? Maybe I just don't get it. I look back at Spencer and glance down, I can see his hard-on through his dress pants. I giggle because it's not like him to get worked up over a chick. He is cocky, but never worked up.

"Why don't you request some VIP treatment?" I ask with a devious smile.

"Nah, I'm good." Spencer glares back at me. Two can play this game. I eye his erection with no shame.

"Little Worthington wants some attention though."

"What? Don't call my cock that."

I throw my head back, laughing hysterically. I so enjoy getting him all riled up. Just then an idea comes to mind.

"Excuse me," I state before getting up and heading to where I hope someone can help me.

I return minutes later and smile at Spencer. He going to kill me. It's not usually like me to do something like this either. It's just I'm kind of sick of following Daddy's rules and being on my best behavior. I needed to do something, slightly wild.

"You can thank me later." I wink.

"For what?"

"You'll see." I turn away from Spencer's questioning eyes and that's when I notice him. All dark and handsome. Holy hell is he hot, and shit if he is not walking up to our table.

"Mr. Worthington?" Oh my, even his voice is sexy. He looks at me, his dark stare holds me in place. It's as if there's no one else in this club. Just him and me.

"That's me," Spencer states, not seeming to care. He barely turns to look at the guy. Too bad I can't say the same.

"You've requested Lettie in the gold lounge, she'll be ready in a few minutes."

Oh my god, he works here. Shit! I continue staring at this beautiful creature, how can I not? He has dark, messy hair. The kind women want to run their fingers through. His eyes are darker than the night sky and the silver hoop in his lip screams bad boy.

I pay no attention as Spencer speaks. Don't care. I'm too busy studying this man. He is dressed professionally; his black buttoned-down shirt doesn't have one wrinkle. His sleeves are rolled up to his elbows, exposing many tattoos. They run from his wrist up. I should not be looking at this man, he is all wrong for me. Not my type. However, staring back at him, I could get lost in his eyes and I almost do until I hear Spencer clear his throat.

"Charla?"

I break contact with the tatted-up bad boy and look at my best friend. He's giving me a questioning look; I already know he will ask me about this later.

"I figured you might enjoy a little show." I shrug my shoulders to play off just being caught checking out a guy I most definitely should not be checking out—and I definitely should not be eyeing his lip piercing.

"If you'll follow me, I'll show you to the lounge," the hot as sin man tells Spencer while I just sit there in awe of his presence.

"Yeah, sure." Spencer glares at me as he gets up. I just smile and turn my attention to the cologne I just got a whiff of as the bad boy walks past. I take note of his ass. It sure looks good in those pants. Shit.

With the two of them gone, I feel a little lonely. I'm going to need another drink to pass the time.

And while I sip my drink, I silently hope to find those dark eyes again. Even if they mean trouble.

3

EAST

I leave Scarlett with the tool and head to the bar. Rian is serving a few men, so I wait off to the side and glance to the spot where the beautiful blonde bombshell sits. She sticks out like a sore thumb. She doesn't belong here. Why she is here baffles me. If that Worthington guy isn't her boyfriend, why is she even here? So many questions run through my mind. I shouldn't even care one bit. They are paying, nothing else matters. I watch carefully as she looks around the club, probably taking it all in. I wonder what she thinks of my club.

"See something you like, boss?"

I turn to Rian, who nods in the blonde's direction.

"No."

"Uh-huh. Can I get you a water?"

"Yes." I do not attempt to explain myself. I don't need to. I can't be interested in someone I don't know. That's not how I roll and besides, I have no time to get to know anyone, nor do I want to.

Rian comes back with a bottle of water and hands it to me before going back to tend the bar. He's my best bartender and he knows it. It's why I allow him to get away with his remarks.

I take a sip and turn to look at that corner of the club once more. I'm a little shocked to see her looking my way; well, she was. She clearly knows I just caught her by how quickly she looked away. She stares out at the stage and the lights hit her cheeks just right, they are a shade of pink. She almost looks familiar, but I can't place where I may have seen her before. One thing I'm certain of is that I haven't fucked her. I would have remembered her.

"Why don't you go say hello?"

Without turning to my nosey ass bartender, I reply, "Drop it, Rian." He should be focusing more on the customers and less on me.

I walk off with my water and decide to do a check to make sure everything is as it should be. I rarely have issues here. I take pride in this place, as it was my grandfather's before I took it over. I changed a lot, for the better. More security and cameras to protect us. A limit on how much alcohol a customer can purchase and not letting scum in here. My grandfather let anyone in, but not me. Nope.

It took me about two years to clean this place up and make it what it is today. No one, and I mean no one, will ruin what I've built.

After doing my checks and touching base with Marc, I decide to check on the bombshell. She seems bored while looking at her phone as I quietly walk up.

"Not happy here?"

She drops her phone on the table; clearly, I've startled her.

"What? Oh my, um... no..."

"Don't sugarcoat, I already know you don't want to be

here." I do. It's written all over her face. Why she paid for VIP treatment for her friend blows my mind.

"You do? It's just... this really isn't my scene."

No shit.

"What is your scene?"

I watch as she thinks about what to say. I can almost bet she's about to lie to me.

"I don't really have a scene." She shrugs her shoulders.

"I find that hard to believe, I'm sorry I didn't catch what your name was."

"It's Charla." She sticks her hand out instantly for me to shake.

The minute I place my hand in hers, I feel it, the electricity. It's unlike anything I've ever felt. Not that I feel much these days, I'm pretty numb. This feeling, it's strange. She must feel it too, her green eyes go wide.

"It's nice to meet you, Charla." I allow her name to roll slowly off my tongue, liking how it sounds.

"Are you going to tell me your name?"

She's got bite, I'll give her that. "East Sinclair, owner of The Red Society."

"Oh!"

Knew that was coming. It shocks most people to learn I own this strip club. I probably look more like a thug than I do a wealthy businessman. People and their stereotyping used to piss me off, but not anymore though. They can fuck off with that shit. I am a very successful business owner, and if I want to be covered in tattoos and body piercings, that's my choice.

"I get that often," I smirk.

"I'm sorry, I didn't mean to sound like that, it's just I deal with businessmen daily and they are all the same, clean cut, and not one thing out of place."

"Sounds boring."

Charla giggles."It can be, I suppose."

"Guess I'm the first businessman who isn't boring."

She smiles and then there's silence. It's awkward. I make a snap decision to do something I've never done.

"Can I buy you a drink?"

I hope I don't regret this offer. Fuck, what is wrong with me? Of course, I'm going to regret this.

"Martini, please." Charla smiles at me.

I nod once, not wanting to leave her presence, but I need space to get my shit together.

Rian has a shit-eating grin when I approach. That fucker has probably been keeping an eye on me.

"East, man, you never— "

"Stop." I firmly cut him off from speaking. "Get me a Martini."

"Ah, shit." Rian laughs and shakes his head as he goes about his task. The minute he goes to set the glass down, I grab it out of his hands and head back to Charla.

To my surprise, Worthington is standing in front of their table and he is helping Charla out of her seat. I stop and check my watch; he should still be in with Scarlett. What the hell?

In a few quick strides, I make my way to the two of them.

"Charla? Mr. Worthington?"

"East, I mean Mr. Sinclair, we were just leaving. It was a pleasure to speak with you."

Seriously? She's gone all prim and proper on me? She won't even make eye contact with me. I look at Worthington, who is staring at Charla.

"Were you not satisfied, Mr. Worthington?" I try to direct his attention back to me. I want to know why he's not with Scarlett still. Not to mention he has interrupted my conversation with Charla.

"The dance was fine; we just have to be going is all. I left her extra since cutting her time short."

Tilting my head, I study him. No man, and I mean no man, has ever left a private show early. Not while I've owned this place. I've had to have men escorted out because they refused to leave when their time was up. Something isn't sitting right with me on this, I need to speak with Scarlett.

"Very well then." I wave my hand toward the exit. "I hope you return another time, you as well, Charla."

I don't know why I said that last part, it just slipped out.

Charla's face heats, and I can feel Worthington's eyes on me. I don't bother to look at him. I don't give a fuck about what he is thinking. I turn and start to walk away before pausing to turn around.

"Have a nice evening," I smirk before walking off without so much as a glance back. Truth be told, I couldn't care less if that guy returns. Charla though is welcome back whenever. I don't know why I find her intriguing; I just do.

My next stop is Scarlett. I hope like hell she didn't fuck up. She never has before, but there's a first time for everything.

4

CHARLA

"What was that about, Charla?" Spencer drills me the minute we get in my Lexus. I knew he would, so I decide to play dumb.

"What?"

"You and him, what's up with that?"

"Me and him... the owner? You can't be serious. Absolutely nothing there. He just happened to be walking by the table and stopped to make sure I was enjoying his club."

From the corner of my eye, I watch Spencer as he rubs his jaw. Not an ounce of stubble. He's always clean-shaven. Unlike East. If I had to guess, it's been a few days since he shaved. I'd be lying if I said it wasn't hot. Why am I still thinking about East?

"Charla?"

"What? Yes, sorry, Spence."

"Exactly, you are too busy thinking about him."

"I am not."

I shake my head as I put the car in reverse.

"Oh yeah? Then why did he have a drink for you in his hand when he walked up to us?"

Shit.

"Why did you leave your private dance early?" I ask, needing to change the subject.

I'm grateful that I have to focus on the road and not Spencer's stare. I can practically feel his eyes on me, assessing me. I hate it. I hate being judged.

"Well?"

"I didn't want a dirty stripper all over me."

"Oh, come on! The strip club was your idea. I'm not buying it."

"Just drop it, Charla."

I can't be certain, but I feel like he's pissed off over the situation or that he's not telling me the truth.

"Spence—"

"I said drop it."

The rest of the drive is filled with suffocating silence. I don't bother to respond to Spencer's question and he doesn't push. He also doesn't answer my question either. As much as I want to hear about his private dance with the stripper, I am not about to pry anymore than I already have.

After parking my sexy beast in the parking garage, we both head up to our condos. Yup, we live in the same building.

While we live in the same beachside condominium, he is on the tenth and top floor. I'm on the seventh. Spencer's penthouse is just that. He had to have the best of the best, and the perfect view. Meanwhile, I couldn't have cared less, but Daddy pays for it even though I can afford it on my own. Yes, I guess I'm spoiled. I mean I have tried to make my payment multiple times. Each time, my father had already paid for it, so I stopped trying.

Ugh, my father. Thinking about him and the recent events that have transpired dampen my mood. He has so much control over me, and I need to figure out how to change that. I'm an adult.

Once in my door, I drop my keys in the porcelain dish by the front door and kick off my heels, not caring where they land. I go straight for the fridge. I need a bottle of wine and a shower.

After pouring a glass of pink Moscato, not caring that I'm mixing alcohol, I head to my room. It's massive and there is white carpet throughout. I've left the curtains open so that the moonlight shines in. Walking over to the French doors, I stare out at the ocean. The moonlight is beaming off the dark waters of the Atlantic Ocean. The sounds of the waves crashing over and over begin to soothe me. I'll admit, this view never gets old. It always takes my breath away and makes me feel at peace. I stand there, staring out, and allow my thoughts to go to East Sinclair, the dark hair, dark eyed, bad boy. He's all wrong for me, yet for some reason, I can't get him out of my head. Maybe it's because he's different from all of the other businessmen I'm used to dealing with. I allow my mind to drift to places it shouldn't. I wonder what the darkness would be like. I take a sip of wine; surely East knows how to satisfy a woman. He owns a strip club, after all. I wonder if he sleeps with the strippers too. Most likely. Ugh. *Enough, Charla.*

I pad my way to my bathroom and start the shower, turning it to the hottest setting.

As I undress down to my black lace bra and thong, I stare at myself in the mirror. Is this what men would see if I were on stage dancing? I like to think I have a decent figure. My breasts are a c-cup, not too large or too small. I have a little bit of an ass.

"What would East see?" I whisper out loud before shaking my head. That's a silly question. I barely know the man, and the chances of ever seeing him again are pretty slim.

I give myself one last look before removing the rest of my clothes and stepping into the shower.

The water stings my skin immediately. Good. I need to feel something. I start washing my face, letting the perfect image of who I am run down the drain.

Will I ever find the real Charla Krauss? Or will I forever live in Daddy's shadow?

I am still wound up as I get out of the shower and wrap myself up in my silky robe. The hot water did very little to ease any tension. Maybe pleasuring myself will help. It's been a while since I've last had sex with Corey and that was less than satisfying.

Walking to my four-poster king size bed that is covered in pink satin sheets, I reach into the side table drawer. I look at my options even though I already know which one I'll choose. My pink vibrator. It's my favorite and gets the job done.

Once seated up by the pillows and comfortable, I unhook my robe, letting it fall open to expose my bare skin. After adjusting the intensity, I slowly touch myself with my fingers before inserting my trusty, pink vibe.

The sensation causes my head to instantly fall back. There is a reason this is my favorite, it hits my g-spot and clit just right.

Closing my eyes, I picture him while slowly moving my vibrator, teasing myself. I imagine his mouth on me and how his stubble would feel against my skin. How his lip piercing would feel against my pussy. My legs begin to tremble as I crave more. I need more.

Keeping my mind on East Sinclair, I think about how his hands would feel all over me as I begin to pinch and pull at my nipple with my free hand. Thoughts of him touching me in ways that would only happen behind a closed door pushes me closer to the edge.

I'm so close, I hold my pink toy still allowing the vibration to assault my clit with no end in sight. My toes start to curl and know it will only be seconds before let go so, I picture black eyes between my thighs, sucking my clit until I finally shatter.

Dark eyes still haunt me as the shockwaves fade. I roll over and start to drift off, still thinking about the bad boy without a care in the world about anything else.

5

CHARLA

A few weeks have come and gone since I've seen those black eyes that constantly creep into my thoughts, mostly when I'm touching myself. Lately, I can't seem to wait to get home to lock myself away in my room where I can be alone with such thoughts. It makes me feel dirty, yet I can't resist.

Not tonight though, tonight my dearest father is having a meet and greet event for Corey and his upcoming campaign. My father is endorsing Corey to be the next mayor and is hosting tonight so that Corey gets good exposure with some of the local big wigs along with some of the businesses.

Me, being the perfect daughter I am, must be in attendance. I'm dreading it because I'm expected to be sweet toward Corey. Just being in his presence makes me feel nauseous and know I will hate every bit of it.

There will be cameras everywhere too. Yup, my father invited the press. Anything to up that exposure. His goal is to get enough businesses to back Corey. Having this event is supposed to secure that. Whatever, if they knew the real

Corey, they would not be endorsing him. It's a sick thing to have to pretend he's a good guy. I know I will not personally be endorsing the sexist pig. If I could, I would warn people to run the other way. But I can't. That's not the lady I was raised to be.

I'm strapping on my black heels when I hear the latch click on my front door. Spencer. Yes, he has a key.

"Char, you ready?"

"In a minute," I shout from my closet.

"Come on, we're going to be late and Mr. Krauss won't stand for that."

"Coming," I say even though I don't care about being late. My father won't make a scene in front of the community. The verbal beating will happen behind closed doors later. That I can handle.

"Charla! Let's go!" Spencer hollers from the foyer. He can't stand to be late in front of my father. He has to maintain the perfect image and all that bullshit. It makes me groan.

"Wow!" Spencer says as he looks me up and down. Thankfully, he is my best friend and the gesture doesn't make me feel uncomfortable.

"You're not so bad looking either."

Spencer is dressed in navy khakis and a light blue dress shirt with a tie that accents both colors nicely.

"All eyes are going to be on you, especially Corey's." Spencer's eyes narrow. "Maybe you should change right quick."

"Don't be silly, I'll be fine, now let's go." I reach my arm out for Spencer to take, and he does without another word.

My red dress falls just above my knees. It fits like a glove, hugging my hips and ass perfectly. It has a scoop neck that keeps it classy. I added a pearl necklace and matching earrings to give it the perfect touch. I glance in the mirror as we walk past. I do look hot. I put my hair up in a high bun. I did my makeup a little darker, adding a smoky eye and a nude lip stain. Classy with a side of sexy is what I call it. The hell with what everyone will think or whisper. For the first time in a long time, I'm dressed for me and no one else.

Spencer gets us to the hotel convention center in record time. Upon entering the doors, we are both handed flutes filled with champagne. No shocker there, I think to myself. I feel cameras on me already. It makes me feel a little on edge. I hate to be in the spotlight without my knowledge. There is just something about having my pictures taken without my consent that doesn't sit right with me.

"There's your father, we best make our way over to say hello so he knows that you have arrived."

I nod and down my drink. I'm going to need more champagne to get through tonight's bullshit alive. I glance around for a waiter and spot one instantly.

"All right, Spence, let's go see my father." I grab a flute and continue on my way. I notice my father's back is now to us, he's talking to someone, but his large figure blocks who it is. Not that I care, I just need to say hello and then find a table to sit at so I can sulk in silence and plaster on a smile when needed.

Spencer chuckles at me. He knows me well enough to know I'm drinking to numb the bullshit. It's why he drove tonight.

"Father," I say sweetly as I plaster on my fake, yet perfect smile.

"Ah, Charla, Spencer, I was wondering when you two would get here." He leans down and places a quick kiss on my cheek, then shakes Spencer's hand.

And so it begins.

Keeping eyes on my father, I continue smiling while biting my tongue.

"Where are my manners, let me introduce you to—" He directs his attention to the person he was talking to before we walked up, and I'll be damned.

East Sinclair is standing before me. The man that has haunted my thoughts for the past few weeks. Those same darker than dark eyes that I picture every time I pleasure myself are looking back at me, clearly just as shocked as I am.

My father clears his throat, a subtle warning to me.

"Yes, sorry, it is a pleasure to meet you." I stick my hand out to shake his and pray like hell that he can't feel my heart rate that just spiked. His touch shocks me, sending electricity down my spine. How can a stranger make me feel like this?

"Likewise, Miss Krauss." Even his voice vibrates throughout my body. No one has ever spoken my name the way he just did.

All too soon though, he lets go of my hand and reaches for Spencer's.

"East Sinclair, I believe we've met before, Mr. Worthington, is it?" East winks.

Oh my God! It dawns on me, does my father know what kind of business East owns? If so, he's going to know Spencer went there. Shit.

"I believe we have met, call me Spencer," Spencer grits out, his face void of any emotion. I know him though, and I know he is not pleased to see East. However, Spencer is an expert at masking emotions. He gives nothing away.

My father claps his hands together. "Ah, you two have met, wonderful. Charla, Mr. Sinclair is a successful business owner who is here tonight to see what Corey Richards has to offer the city and the local business owners." He speaks proudly of Corey; it makes me want to vomit. I don't. Instead, I smile like the shit that spews from my father's mouth is the greatest thing he has ever said.

"I'm sure you have plenty of great things to tell Mr. Sinclair about Corey. They are very close." My father squeezes my arm. While I'm sure it looks to be done in a loving manner, I know the real reason behind it.

A warning to not fuck this up.

"Spencer, my boy, would you mind joining me in making sure the stage is set and ready?" Father always demands that Spencer help make sure these things go off without issue. I hate that he uses Spencer, but he would never speak out against him. It's quite sad.

"Yes, sir." Spencer eyes me cautiously. He doesn't want to leave me alone with East. "If you'll excuse me, we'll return shortly."

"I look forward to continuing talking to you, Mr. Krauss," East states all professionally as my father and Spencer turn to go.

I'll admit, he's dressed perfectly and blends in. He has a black blazer on, his black dress shirt is pressed allowing the blood-red tie he's wearing to stand out. There isn't a single wrinkle in his slacks. Yes, I looked. How could I not? His tattoos are covered and I don't see his lip ring. A stranger would never guess that his arms are covered in tattoos that stop at his wrists.

"See something you like?"

No, he didn't just call me out. I can feel my face heat and unlucky for me, the lights are not turned down low.

"You're blushing." East flashes me a teasing smile and I swear I can feel myself becoming wet.

"Why are you here?" I ask, needing to turn the attention from me.

"I'd ask you the same, except I know now you are here because your father is here."

"You didn't answer my question, why are you here?"

"I'm a business owner, am I not?" He shoots me a questioning look.

I take a sip of my champagne and decide to stay quiet.

"I take it this Corey fellow is your boyfriend; you know, since you two are so close." The words sound sour as they roll off of East's tongue.

I gag, which causes the champagne to go up my nose. "Definitely not my boyfriend. Don't ever make that assumption again."

East rubs his chin slightly while studying me. His eyes are all over me. I silently pat myself on the back regarding the choice of my dress. At least I have that going for me.

"The color of your dress is perfect." He winks as he suddenly takes a step closer to me which causes me to stumble back a step out of pure instinct.

"Something about your body language tells me you don't want to be here, why is that?"

What the hell? How does he do that?

"What?" I decide to play coy.

"You don't want to be here, it's written all over your face. You might have your daddy fooled, but not me." East winks before reaching for my elbow and tugging me. "Walk with me."

"Um... okay." His touch feels like a torch setting my body on fire. I follow his lead while glancing around the room. People will surely see this. If there is one thing I've learned about these events, it is that people love to gossip. They will give the press whatever it is they want. The last thing I need is a front-page scandal. I need to break our contact, however, my feet betray me and continue walking with East, allowing him to keep his hand on me.

We continue walking until we are out in the breezeway. It's cool out this evening. I welcome it. I need something to put out the inferno that is suddenly taking over my body.

We walk to an area that is not well lit, he stops, turns to me, and lets go of my arm. When he lets go, the heat I felt moments before dies instantly.

"Now tell me, why it is you don't want to be here."

"I— "

"Do not lie, Charla."

"Fine, I can't stand Corey."

"I see, what did he do to you to make you feel that way?"

"He thinks because my father adores him that I will become his possession." I huff, no point in lying.

"So, he's a piece of shit?"

"Essentially, yes."

"Noted."

I stare at East's tie, red, like The Red Society. Makes sense now. No wonder he likes the color of my dress.

"What are you thinking about?" He steps closer. This time I don't move.

"Your red tie."

"Is that so?" East reaches for it, pulls it away from his body, then looks at me. "What would you do if I wrapped this around your wrists?"

"Wha..what?"

East steps even closer, bringing his face awfully close to mine. The heat I felt moments ago under his touch returns. I inhale his scent. It is mixture of spearmint and woods.

"You heard me, Charla." His voice is just above a

whisper as he takes the tie and rubs it against my collarbone.

Holy shit.

"Answer me."

"I'm….I'm not sure." It's the truth, kind of. I've never been tied up before and part of me is now intrigued. I won't be telling him that though.

"That's what I thought. You are too pure to want what I have to offer."

The tie falls away from me as East takes a step back, leaving me feeling cold. What is wrong with me? Why am I feeling this way about someone I don't know?

"Tell me more about Corey." East changes the subject back to dirtbag.

"Corey loves money. The more he has, the happier he is. He really only cares about himself."

"What do you care about?"

His question takes me by surprise, causing me to close my eyes to think. I'm not entirely sure and that makes me question what kind of person I am.

"Well?" East asks.

I sigh. "No one has ever asked me that before."

"That's sad, Charla." East's voice sounds sincere and in a way it makes me wonder if he pities me. I hope not.

I've always had to live for my father and maintain the image he demanded. He has always been there for me though. He raised me. My mother was unfit. I should be grateful. Right?

Shrugging my shoulders, I reply, "I care about a lot of things, just nothing in particular."

"You mean you care about yourself and your looks."

"That's not true! Who do you think you are to state such a thing? You don't know me." He's got some nerve, I think as I step forward to walk past him, but he grabs my wrist, pulling me in close again.

"Want to know what I care about?"

"No," I state firmly. I don't care what he has to say.

"Exactly. You only care about yourself, Char-la." East lets go of my wrist, turns, and walks away, leaving me standing there completely confused by what just transpired. Shaking my head, I make my way back inside. I'm sure a few select people are looking for me.

Sure enough, upon entering Corey is standing there as if waiting for me.

"Charla." He glares at me.

"Hi, Corey." I don't feel like talking to him and continue on my way, hoping he'll leave me alone, but he doesn't. He follows close behind to keep up with my pace.

"We need to talk."

"Not now, Corey."

I'm suddenly halted back into his chest. His death grip on my upper arm both hurts and shocks me.

"Corey! What on earth is your problem?"

"Don't think I didn't see you and that guy outside. What the hell was that about?" His hot breath hits my cheeks. I flinch, not liking that he is so close to me.

"What I do is none of your business, now let me go."

"That's not the answer I expect from you." Corey squeezes my arm tighter, which I didn't think was possible because he's already causing me enough pain.

Squeezing my eyes shut to try to block out the pain, I speak calmly. "Let me go, Corey. My father won't be happy— "

"Charla, is everything okay?"

I recognize his sexy voice and breathe a sigh of relief, yet, when I open my eyes, I see nothing but fury staring straight past me. Eyes on Corey. Rage rolls off of East like the waves crash against the shoreline during a hurricane. He's angry.

"Charla is fine, you can go." Corey speaks for me.

"First, I wasn't talking to you. Second, it is clear by the grip you have on her arm," East points to where Corey still has my arm, "that everything is not fine. Let go of her arm. Now."

Corey doesn't let me go; instead, he tries being manipulative.

"Charla, baby, tell this dude everything is fine and that you like it rough. Don't you, baby?"

I slowly shake my head, he's crazy. Damn crazy.

"I'll tell you one more time to let her go." East steps closer to us. His eyes never leave Corey.

"Or what?" Corey instigates.

"Corey, stop, just let me go." I need to defuse this situation before any cameras come rolling.

"Or I'll make sure the press and police know that you seem to think it's okay to treat a woman in such a way. I doubt you want that, especially with your upcoming campaign."

East tilts his head as if he's waiting for Corey to put up a fight. To my surprise, he doesn't. He lets me go and spins me to face him. He grabs my chin and kisses me hard, forcing his tongue in my mouth. It's so vile that I instantly shove at his chest, forcing him back.

Corey smirks and winks before walking away like shit didn't just happen. I feel myself becoming angry and upset all at once. I will myself not to cry. It's something I learned to control a long time ago. My father didn't like for me to be a crybaby, and well, I just became numb to anything I deemed emotional.

What just happened, though, has me shook. Before I can process any more shit, East is in my face now, gentle hands tilt my chin to look at him.

"Are you all right, Charla?" The same black eyes that were just full of fury moments ago are now full of concern.

I nod my head, for fear of speaking will set off my emotions.

"You're not okay. You're shaking and the look on your face gives you away. Look at your arm. Look at it." His voice is angry again.

I glance down at my right arm, sure enough, purple marks are already forming. Great.

I swallow slowly, before whispering, "I'll be okay. I need to go." My voice nearly breaks.

I do. I need to get out of here. I don't have a coat and can't be seen like this. The press will have a field day.

"Do you have your car?"

Shit. I shake my head. "I came with Spencer."

"Text him, tell him you aren't feeling well and that you called a cab. Come on, I'll have my driver take you home."

Before I can respond, he shrugs out of his blazer and helps me to put it on. I'm speechless. No man has ever been so kind to me aside from Spencer.

"Where is your phone?"

Right, I was supposed to be texting Spencer. I reach into my small handbag and retrieve my phone. I quickly text Spencer while allowing East Sinclair to guide me out. I tell him a sudden migraine has come on, leaving me feeling sick, and that to let my father know I took a cab home.

I allow East to escort me out a set of doors. He's currently on the phone, speaking too quickly for me to understand. I honestly don't care what it is he is saying. He is getting me away from Corey and all the eyes in the room, that's all that matters to me right now.

We walk a little further until a slick, blacked-out Mercedes stops in front of us. East walks up to it and opens the door and immediately helps me in. I notice him looking around before turning his attention back to me and for a split second, I panic thinking someone has just witnessed him and me.

"Burns will take you straight home."

East goes to close the door, but I stop him, "Wait… you're not coming too?"

"Do you want me to?"

"Yes." I look down at my hands, slightly embarrassed. I've never been one to need help, so this is a tad embarrassing for me. "I just don't want to be alone right now."

Silence.

I chance a look at him, he's studying me, his face void of any emotion. He nods once and gets in, closing the door behind him. The sound of the locks makes me a little nervous. I am in a car with a stranger after all, though East doesn't feel like a stranger to me.

"Please give Burns your address."

"Oh, right, yes."

I rattle off my address, then relax back in my seat as the car pulls into traffic. I'm thankful to be getting out of that place.

Closing my eyes, it doesn't take long for me to notice the silence that has taken over. It's nearly suffocating and I can't stand it. I have to force myself to keep my eyes shut and try to think of anything at all aside from the silence.

It doesn't work.

6

CHARLA

East is staring at me when I open my eyes. His gaze is serious, there's a tic in his jaw. Maybe he is angry that he is dealing with me and my bullshit. Maybe he is pissed off with how Corey acted. Either way, it should alarm me, yet it does the complete opposite.

It awakens something in me.

"Why are you staring at me?"

"Trying to figure you out. Why did you allow that pig to touch you?"

"I, I don't know. Lately, it has gotten worse, and I just think he thinks I'll cave and submit to him." I shrug my shoulders, trying to play it off like it's no big deal. The reality is, I know it is a big deal. Corey leaving marks is a huge red flag. I'm just not sure how to approach the matter. That's a problem for another day.

I decide to pull my hair down because I can't take it being in such a tight bun any longer, I lean forward and shake my hair out. When I sit back, I notice the strained look on East's face as his nose flares.

"You shouldn't let people dictate your life. It'll destroy you from the inside."

I nod, truer words have never been spoken to me. He's not wrong. These issues with my father, and even Corey, have been consuming me more and more lately. Even Spencer has been warning me that their behavior is unhealthy.

East shakes his head. "I see it daily. The women who work for me, most of them are stuck and being controlled. It's why they strip and dance. I give them a safe place to not only work, but to be free for a couple of hours."

"Wow, I had no idea."

"I know. You are spoiled. You live this fabricated life while silently being controlled. You have to see that, Charla."

"I do... now." And I do. Tonight confirms it. Things need to change. I look down at my arm and study the bruising.

"Does it hurt?"

I shrug in response. It does a little bit, I just rather not focus on that. I look up to East and stare into his eyes.

"Thank you."

Then I do something I've never done before. I lean over quickly and kiss East on the lips. He doesn't pull away, but I can feel how tense he is in his seat, no longer relaxed. I don't pull back though, instead, I dare myself to test the turbulent waters by sticking my tongue out just a little to see if he'll open up. The minute I do, he opens and kisses me back. It's electrifying. It's intense and carnal.

I lose myself in the moment while our tongues dance amongst the flames of our desire. I scoot closer to him, needing more. He kisses me hard. I've never been kissed in such a way.

Corey never kissed me like this.

East is the first to break our kiss. My lips miss his on mine already.

"Charla," he growls while staring at me through heated eyes. It sends chills down my spine to the point that I don't bother with a response. Instead, I make a snap decision and climb on his lap and straddle him. A surprised expression takes over his face. I surprise myself too. My dress is now riding up my thighs, a few more inches and I would be exposing the satin thong that is currently covering my most private area.

Not caring, I place my lips back on his. I like the way they feel there. I pull back just enough to whisper, "I'm sick of being the good girl, I want to be bad, just for tonight."

"Charla."

East's words vibrate off my lips, the sensation sends a shockwave straight down to my core.

I want him.

Before I realize it, I'm raking my hands through his dark hair, I can't help but get lost in East Sinclair.

When the connection between our lips is lost, I feel it. I feel lost. I open my eyes and East looks like he is in pain. His eyes have turned darker and his hands are at his sides balled into fists, veins bulging.

"What's wrong?"

"We shouldn't do this; you don't want me."

"What if I do?" I raise my eyebrow, slightly annoyed with this cat and mouse game.

"Charla, I'm not what you need, trust me."

"What I need is to just forget about everyone and every-thing for one night."

I probably sound desperate, however, it's been a shit evening and I just want a real man to touch me for once.

Reaching out, I slide my fingers through his tie while

gauging his reaction. I can't be certain but the way he swallows ever so slowly is a sign that he is fighting this, whatever it is between us.

"Come on, East, let me just forget for a little while."

His lips crash into mine hard. Our tongues dance wildly as I grab for his shirt while he grips my bare thighs. Everywhere he touches me sizzles. Feeling him hardening beneath me turns me on further. I slowly begin to grind on his lap. God, I've missed this feeling, the friction. I need more.

I moan out in pleasure as I feel East slide his hand further up my thigh until his finger skims the satin. His touch ignites me. It makes me feel alive.

As he continues tracing the lace, teasing me, someone clears their throat, causing us to both go dead still.

"Yes, Burns?" East asks, voice strained.

"We've arrived at Ms. Krauss's residence."

"Thank you."

East looks from the driver to me. "You're blushing."

I was so lost in us that I forgot we weren't alone. Biting my bottom lip, I just shrug.

East leans back in the seat and looks me up and down. His eyes pause when they reach between my thighs, where his fingers still rest. So close, yet so far away.

"Let me walk you to your door."

His words shock me and slightly offend me. I was hoping this was going somewhere, now I'm not so sure.

Giving him my signature, fake smile, I quickly pull my dress down and slide off of his lap. I wait for him to step out of the car first and then like the gentleman he is, holds his hand out for me to take while climbing out. I appreciate the gesture even though he has me wound up so tight.

The walk to my door is quiet, neither of us says a single

word. I guess we are pretending like nothing happened back there in that car. Pulling my keys out, I smile at the man in front of me. "Thank you for coming to my aid tonight."

East just nods in response, which is both annoying and confusing.

"Can I invite you in?"

"I don't think that's a good idea, Charla."

"Why not?"

"Again, I'm not what you need, and you are not going to like what I have to offer."

I step closer so that I'm toe to toe with him and place my hands on his chest.

"Listen, I'm not asking for any sort of commitment. I just want to get lost, let's just pretend for tonight." I whisper that last part in hopes to sway him to just come in. I'm wet and more than desperate for a real release.

"You really don't want to do this, not with me."

"Oh, but I do."

"I don't do sex."

"Care to explain what you mean by that?" Because I'm sure as hell confused.

"I fuck, Charla. No making love, no sweet shit. Straight fucking is what I do. I don't even kiss. What happened in the car was a simple lapse in judgment."

"Oh..." I'm left speechless.

"I told you that you don't want this."

East steps back and turns to leave.

"Wait." I sound desperate, yet I don't care. I am.

He turns and gives me a questioning look.

"Fuck me... just for tonight."

"Charla."

He doesn't finish speaking because I've started unzipping the back of my dress, which causes the straps to fall nearly enough to expose the top of my breasts. I don't care that I'm standing in my doorway and that other people could possibly witness this, especially the eyes behind the security cameras.

"Fucking hell," East growls before pulling me into my suite.

I smile, almost excited to be doing this for all the wrong reasons.

To be doing something risky.

My smile falls fast though the minute I catch the carnal look on East's face.

"We are fucking and nothing more, understand?"

"I told you, I'm sick of being the good girl. I want to be bad... for once."

East shakes his head at me and makes work at undoing his tie. The way his hands work at it, nearly makes my mouth water. I can't wait to have his hands on me. On my body.

With his tie now in his hand, he walks away from me, toward my glass French doors. I follow him, not knowing why he has gone over there instead of my bedroom.

"Remove your thong," East speaks while staring out at the dark sea. "Keep your heels and dress on."

I do as he says without question. I want this so bad. Something about East tells me I should run, run far away. Yet here I am, zipping my dress back up and sliding my thong off for him.

East turns to me and grabs my hands, bringing them together. Confusion runs through me for a second until he takes the tie and starts wrapping it around my wrists.

He's tying me up.

With his red tie.

Alarm bells go off in my head and I begin to think that maybe this isn't such a good idea. Especially with a man I hardly know. Yet excitement courses through my veins.

"What are you doing?"

"What's it look like I'm doing?"

I hesitate before answering, "Tying me up?"

"If you know what I'm doing, then why ask?"

East pulls on the tie that is firmly around both wrists, giving it one final tug to make sure it isn't coming undone. It's tight, but not cutting my circulation off tight. Thank God for that.

"I meant why are you tying me up?"

He smirks, saying nothing as he leads me straight up to the glass panes. He turns me and presses my body up against the window. It's cold. He takes both of my hands and places them above my head, then spreads my legs apart.

A low grow comes from his throat before he speaks, "This is how I fuck. I don't need you touching me or kissing me. Take it or leave it."

As soon as the last words leave his mouth, he inserts a finger into me hard. It causes me to jump. Naturally, I go to bring my arms down, forgetting that they are tied up, but East grabs them, keeping them in place.

He keeps pumping a finger into me roughly. Seconds of pain followed by undeniable pleasure. The sweet mixture of the two is something I'll gladly take more of.

My head falls back as East continues to dive a finger into my soaked pussy while teasing my clit with another. It's been so long without a real man's touch. I may combust just from his fingers alone.

"Take it or leave it, Charla," East breathes from behind

my ear. His sinister voice leaves chills down my spine. I should take it as a warning.

But I won't.

His fingers continue working their magic. I start to feel myself inch closer to the edge. All those nights of touching myself while picturing him could never add up to how good he is currently making me feel.

"Answer me." East stops suddenly, pulling his fingers back, just enough to leave me on a tightrope, desperately wanting to fall free, straight down into a world of bliss.

I groan out in frustration. "Come on, East," Seriously, I need him to move his fingers.

"I need to hear you say it."

"Fine. I take it, there. Satisfied?"

Without another word, he dips his finger back in roughly, working my clit until my tight rope snaps.

I fall.

And boy do I fall.

I fall so far that I begin to worry no other will ever make me feel as good as East Sinclair just made me feel with his fingers.

"Holy shit..." I pant out while resting my face on the glass, thankful for the cool down. My legs go weak from trembling, but East is there and quickly wrapping his arms around my waist to keep me from collapsing.

I hear him behind me unzipping his slacks and the sound of a foil wrapper.

Thank goodness he thought of protection because it wasn't even a thought after that orgasm.

"Spread your legs farther." It's a statement and one I follow promptly without question.

East's hands glide up my dress, pulling it up as he goes. It exposes my bare ass and he slaps it hard one time, causing me to yelp. He quickly rubs where it stings and I have to admit, the sensation has me kind of wanting him to repeat what he just did.

"This is just a fuck, Charla," East growls at me as I feel him line his cock up at my entrance.

"Just fuck me already," I spit back. I don't know why he keeps reminding me. All I need is this one night. Even if he knows how to touch me just the way I like, he is not what I need in my life. *My perfect life.*

The second he thrusts into me, all coherent thoughts go out the window. He's rough. So rough as he pounds into me. I already know that by the time we're finished I will be bruised and so sore. For some reason, just the thought of him leaving his mark on me excites me. Seriously, something must be wrong with me.

East grips my hips while continuing to fuck me. Marking me unlike any man before him. No one has ever fucked me like that, wait let me rephrase that, no one has ever just fucked me. It has always been sex and nothing more. I'm consumed by the pleasurable pain that only East knows how to give. What we are doing is crude to the point it should make me feel dirty. It does but in the best possible way.

It's not long before I feel myself climbing that tight rope again, needing a release that only he knows how to give.

"East..." I moan, my breath fogging the window. If people are out walking the beach and happen to pass by, there's no doubt they would get quite the show. I panic slightly at the thought of someone seeing us... together... in such a way. I nearly go still.

"Stop thinking, Charla," East grits out while gripping me harder, bringing my attention back to him, us.

He reaches up and unzips my dress a little before

reaching around the front and yanking it down. I send a silent plea that he doesn't rip my dress because I certainly like this one.

That plea is quickly forgotten as East grabs my left nipple and pinches it.

Hard.

"Fuck!" I shout out in pain.

East stops pinching my nipple and lightly tugs on it, sending shockwaves straight to my core. It's too much, yet not enough and I once again try to bring my arms down only to remember that they are tied up.

East continues the sweet assault on my nipples while pounding into me in one steady motion. I can't handle it, and not being able to reach out and grab or touch him drives me mad, to the point I can hardly hold on any longer.

"Are you ready?" Easts growls in my ear.

I'm too far gone to speak until he dead stops.

"Answer me."

Why is he like this, I wonder. Always demanding a response from me.

"Charla?"

"Yes!" I snap. I hate how he plays with me like this.

East starts his rhythm back up. He's relentless and takes everything from me without so much as a care. I'm okay with it too. Don't ask why. I just am.

I feel myself stepping off the ledge. He must feel it too because he pinches my erect nipple hard and doesn't let go.

It causes me to fall, and I don't just fall. I dive right into the ocean of ecstasy.

Seconds later, East thrusts into me harder than he was prior before he stills. He's careful as he pulls out of me, holding on to me firmly so I don't crash to the floor. My legs are jello and between my legs is the sweetest pain I've ever felt.

I've been thoroughly fucked.

The amount of pleasure East just handed me is something I know I'll want over and over, and that has trouble written all over it.

"Where's your bathroom?"

"Um... down the hall." I nod in the direction because my hands are still tied up.

East says nothing as he makes sure I'm steady before walking off. When he comes back a few minutes later, I notice he is cleaned up and dressed as if nothing has happened.

He guides me to my room and into the bathroom where he sits me down on the toilet. I watch as he starts the shower, still without saying a word. I study his face, searching for any sign of emotion. Nothing. East doesn't even look at me as he finally begins to untie my wrists. There's an unreadable expression in those black eyes.

Once free, I instantly rub each one where the tie was firmly tied. They are sore, but it's not like a painful sore. I hate to admit the fact that I kind of liked it, being tied up that is.

Glancing back to East, he is still void of any emotion. He was clear about what tonight was and I'm not quite sure how to take that. I've never just done one-night stands.

East turns and walks toward the door that leads back to my room.

"Where are you going?" I ask, even though I already know the answer.

He turns back and looks at me, his eyes refuse to meet mine still.

"I fuck. That is it."

I sit there in shock as he walks out without another word. Once I hear the front door shut, I stand and remove my clothing before carefully stepping into the shower. I shouldn't be shocked. After all, East was clear when he said we were just going to fuck. I agreed to it. Willingly.

And I would agree to it again.

There's no doubt.

I gently wash away any evidence of what happened between us. I'm sore to the touch already. East may be all wrong for me, but the things he did to my body I am certain I'll want to do again.

7

CHARLA

I hear a quick knock on my door followed by the sound of the lock turning. Spencer.

Shit.

He's coming to check on me. I'm in nothing but a satin black nightie, nothing else. I was too sore to bother with a pair of panties and since I sleep alone, I can go without.

Last night with East is still very fresh in my mind and just the thought of how he had his way with me has me squeezing my thighs together.

"Charla!"

"In here," I barely holler back as I sit up in the center of my huge bed.

In storms Spencer, with two coffees in hand.

"Spill now," he demands as he hands me a coffee.

I take a sip, just the way I like it. Loaded with cream, sugar, and caramel flavoring. Some might say I'm spoiled and they would be right.

"Well, I'm waiting."

Oh, right.

"What is there to spill? I wasn't feeling well." A smile

plays on my lips, hidden by my coffee mug as I think of East's fingers on my nipples.

"I'm not daft, Charla. I know you left with that jerk from the club."

"And how would you know that I in fact did?"

"Corey might have mumbled something about it to your father while I was standing there with him."

This just turned sour.

Very sour. It's worse than biting straight into a fresh lemon.

"That's what I thought, now tell me what's going on?"

I shake my head. "Corey was being Corey and he happened to grab me." I point to my bruised arm which causes Spencer's eyes to go wide. I watch the tic in his jaw. "It just so happens that he did it in front of the owner of the club." I pause taking a deep breath before continuing, "Mr. Sinclair came to my aid and since I was upset over the ordeal, he offered me a ride home and I took it. I didn't want to face the cameras or anyone else."

There, it's the truth, mostly.

"Shit, Char. Corey is way out of line. This has to stop. You need to speak up."

Spencer reaches out and rubs my arm in sympathy. I hate it and it makes me feel dirty.

"I know," I whisper, knowing full well I probably won't say a word because that's not how Charla Krauss was raised. I know my place.

Even if it is wrong.

Even if I hate it.

———

My phone goes off inside of my desk drawer. I ignore it and continue with my work. There's no time for distractions right now. We need to seal this account. Spencer is counting on me. I can't fuck this up. Not that I have ever screwed up an account I was given. And while I'm certain Spence would never fire me, I don't cut corners with my work. I do my job and I do it well.

So, when my phone goes off again and again, I silently curse and save what I'm working on. Who the hell needs me so bad?

Pulling my phone out, I unlock it to several notifications.

My father.

I groan in frustration as I call him back. He answers on the second ring.

"Charla, why haven't you been answering my calls?" His voice is laced with anger and that only annoys me further.

"I do have a job. I was working."

"Pfft, you don't need to work. I take care of you and once you are married Corey, he will take care of you."

I roll my eyes. "Father, I want to work, I enjoy what I do. And as much as this may upset you, I will not be marrying that man." I can't even say his name, just the thought of him has bile rising in my throat.

"Corey is a good man. You would be a fool not to marry him."

For some reason, his words crack something inside of me.

"No, you would be a fool to force such a pig on me."

"What did you just say to me? Young lady, what's gotten into you? I raised you better."

"That's just it, you did, and Corey is not the man for me. I need you to see that."

I wish I could make him see that asshole the way I see him. I'm afraid it's useless though. Corey is perfect in my father's eyes.

"He is a stable man. You need a stable man in your life. I won't be around forever, and I refuse for you to settle for less."

"Who said I'm settling for less?"

"Anyone that is not Corey will most likely be less."

See, absolutely fucking pointless. Corey is a god in my father's eyes.

"I need to get back to work, was there a reason you needed me?" My words are clipped. I can't help it. I'm pissed off with being interrupted at work and over some sleazeball.

"Don't take that tone with me. The reason for my call was because Corey would like to see you at dinner tonight. I think tonight is the night he wants to make you official. You need to dress presentable and be at the house by eight o'clock."

His words burn into my ear and yet I can't make them make sense. What in the hell is happening right now? I look around my office as everything starts to blur.

"Charla? Are you there?"

Somehow, I manage to reply. What I said, I have no idea.

"Did you hear everything I said? Dress appropriately and do not be late." He ends the call without another word. That's probably a good thing because I'm on the verge of screaming.

Why won't he listen to me? Why doesn't he understand that I do not want to marry Corey Richards?

Not now.

Not ever.

The thought of being his wife makes me sick. So sick that I grab my wastebasket and spill the contents of my lunch into it.

8

EAST

I can't fucking concentrate. A certain blonde has been stuck in my head, and I don't know what to do about it. No woman distracts me.

Never.

So why now?

I don't fucking know. Thoughts of the other night are still fresh in my mind. How easily she gave herself to me. She let me tie her hands. The thought alone has my dick jumping in my slacks.

Fuck.

I hit a button on my computer, switching over to the security cameras. It's early and the employees are still arriving. Rian is going over inventory. Everything is as it should be.

Except for my thoughts.

Charla reacted better than I could have ever imagined. The pain I gave her only turned her on more. Her pussy was soaked, which only allowed me to thrust in and out harder, deeper. Shit. I try to shake these thoughts but now I have a raging hard-on. Grabbing it, I try to think of anything but her.

All thoughts go back to Charla. Her bare pussy was so divine. And that's saying a lot. I've fucked plenty before her, but the way she moved for me. The way she allowed me to pound into her relentlessly.

Without realizing it, I've got my fly down, releasing my dick. I need a release. I need to get that snobby blonde out of my head. That's it. I stroke myself slowly while skimming the cameras to see who is already here that can help me out.

I'm not above fucking my employees. I've done it plenty. It's consensual and a legal document is signed. I don't play around. I also compensate them beyond what they make in a week on the floor. Call me a piece of shit, call them prostitutes, but work is work, even if it is with the boss.

I continue watching the screen while pumping my dick in my hand. Any one of them will do, but the minute I spot Scarlett, I know she's the one I want.

I hit the button for the dressing room on the intercom, "Scarlett, can I please see you in my office?"

I watch as she stills and looks in the direction of the intercom. She straightens herself before walking over and hitting the button. "Yes, sir. I'll be right up."

I smile, pleased with myself. Scarlett will erase all thoughts of the other night. Reaching for the monitor, I hit the power button. My employees get no insight into what I see or do up here. They don't need to.

A few minutes later, there's a knock at my door. "Sir, you wanted to see me?"

"Come in."

Scarlett looks worried as she walks over to my desk. I

eye her from top to bottom, my dick throbs in my hand under my desk. She is the perfect choice. Her blonde waves fall just past her shoulders. I couldn't care less about the red lace corset she has on. Aside from her tits nearly popping out, I'm not here to play with her body. I just need her mouth.

"Have a seat."

The little bit of material she is wearing is pointless. It's see-through, exposing her bare skin. Hell, maybe I will fuck her. I study her pussy through the mesh material for a second longer. There's no point in that thing. I would suggest wearing nothing on stage, but where is the element in fun with that? Men are stupid. They can clearly see all my employees have to offer. However, a little teasing of pulling the string down their thighs has them throwing dollars.

Every. Single. Time.

Fools. But they pay and that's all that matters.

I nod to the contract that is already out in front of her. Scarlett glances at it and realizes what it is right away. This isn't our first time, and it surely won't be the last.

"Oh, of course, sir." She lifts the black felt top pen with one hand while flipping to the last page with the other.

Once she signs her name away to me, she looks up at me.

I scoot my chair back, allowing her to see just what I want from her. She licks her pink lips instantly. My dick twitches in response.

Scarlett wastes no time coming over to me. She palms me with her hand as she drops to her knees. She knows what I want.

Slowly, she drags her tongue from the base of my dick to the head where she licks up the little bit of precum that has pooled. As soon as her lips envelop my shaft, all thoughts of Charla leave my sadistic mind. Scarlett and her lips are the only thing I focus on.

She takes all of me effortlessly. I watch as her eyes water a little each time the head of my dick hits the back of her throat. I won't lie, I enjoy seeing Scarlett like this, under my control.

Her hand strokes me as she continues bobbing up and down on me. I fist her hair guiding her to move faster as I begin to feel my balls tighten. I'm so close to unloading in Scarlett's mouth when my door suddenly opens and in bursts someone.

A certain blonde.

The one I was trying to forget.

Fuck.

"Charla," I state. How the fuck did she get past security?

"Oh my god!" Shock is evident on her face. "I, I need to go."

"Shut the door, Charla."

She stops at my calm words but doesn't turn to face me. I feel Scarlett pause. I look down at her and hold a finger up. I need a minute.

"I said shut the door."

There's no way she is going to burst into my damn office without an explanation. She doesn't, she just stands there. It's obvious she is unsure of what to do. Let me help her out.

I slide my chair back, forcing Scarlett to release me. Damnit. I was so close. I stand and walk over to Charla. Throbbing cock out and all. I have no shame. She has some damn nerve coming in here.

I walk past her and slam my door shut, locking it. She's going nowhere.

"How did you get past security?"

"Um... that's a complicated story."

"I want to hear it." I squeeze myself and her eyes instantly fall to my dick. She bites her lip in response, which only causes me to smirk. From here her scent is intoxicating. Some sort of floral. I'm certain if I sink my teeth into her neck right now, I would be able to taste it. I don't though. I want answers.

"I want to hear your complicated story."

Charla swallows before speaking. "Well, I came in and asked the guy at the bar where I could find you. He ignored me and so I went to leave, realizing coming here was a bad idea."

"It was. Go on."

"As I was heading for the door, some large man asked me what the hell I was doing and that you requested me. He pointed to your door and told me to get moving before I pissed you off. So here I am."

I stop stroking myself. Requested her? I never did any such thing. I stare at Charla, puzzled. I'm going to have to have a meeting with everyone later. Right now, though, my plans have been interrupted and Charla needs to pay for that.

Grabbing her wrists, I pull her toward where Scarlett is still on her knees. She looks confused as fuck. I just shrug, not caring about her feelings. There are no feelings when it comes to this business.

I reach for my chair and position it just where I want it. Then I sit Charla's ass right down in it. She's in a tight black dress that hides her chest well. She's probably afraid someone will see her, and she doesn't want her plump tits on display.

I return to Scarlett and nod once. Immediately her lips swallow my dick. Fuck. It feels so good.

"I think I should go— "

"You will do no such thing," I grit out. "You will watch. I want your eyes on us the entire time."

"East."

"You heard what I said." I stare at Charla, letting her know I am dead serious.

The minute she swallows slowly, I know she isn't going anywhere. If I'm lucky she'll want to join us soon enough.

My hand tangles in Scarlett's hair again, forcing her to suck faster. I won't be able to last. Having Charla watching is fucking with my head. It shouldn't be turning me on as much as it is. I force myself to look away from her and back to Scarlett. Her mascara is now running down her wet cheeks. My cock hitting the back of her throat is to blame.

"Fuck, Scarlett." I thrust hard, jutting inside her mouth. She swallows every last drop of me too.

When her mouth pops off my dick, I help her stand up. I reach for the tissue box on my desk and wipe her face before turning her around.

"Bend over, Scarlett, your turn."

"That's it, I can't watch anymore." Charla stands abruptly which causes me to walk straight over to her.

"You barge into my office, you will sit your perfect little ass back down." My dick still stands at attention for her to see. Part of me is hoping she'll come play; that is until she slaps me as she storms out of my office.

It stings. I should be pissed at her little outburst, but I'm not. Not even in the slightest. Why is that? Maybe a slap to the face is just what I need to get her out of my system.

I turn my attention back to Scarlett. She is still bent over, waiting for instructions. "Good girl. You'll be rewarded now."

She smiles as I walk back to her and open my side

drawer. Her eyes stayed glued to me. She already knows what I'm pulling out. The heat in her eyes confirms it.

I pull out the first two items I'm looking for and open the cap on the lube. Scarlett eyes the small silver object. She might come off as a scared little mouse and doesn't think I don't notice the way she is squeezing her thighs shut. She fucking wants this.

I decide to test my theory. I insert not one, but two fingers into her dripping wet pussy.

Theory confirmed.

Grabbing the lube, I tip it allowing the jelly-like substance to spill out down her lower back, down her crack, where it needs to be. I give her pussy a little more attention before bringing my hand up between her slick folds to her puckered hole. Scarlett tenses as soon as I insert a finger. I give her a minute before adding a finger to stretch her. She grinds lightly against my desk, little moans escape her mouth. Scarlett likes it dirty. Always has. I've come to assume she uses it as an escape from reality. She was dealt shit cards. But who am I to judge? I just give her what she wants in return for what I wanted.

I slowly remove my fingers and grab the shiny plug that has a rhinestone on the top. I rub it across both cheeks before teasing her with it. It's cold against her skin. Instantly, she sticks her ass out, wanting it.

"Sir, please."

"Please what?"

She wiggles her ass again, so I slap it.

Hard.

"Sir, please give it to me." She yelps in desperate anticipation.

Her words cause my dick to jump. If I don't insert the

plug, I'm going to be inserting my dick and then neither of us will work tonight.

Sighing, I slowly insert the plug. She clamps right down on it.

"Yes, sir. yes." Her words come out in a rush. Maybe fucking her won't be such a bad thing.

Fuck.

No, I can't. Thoughts of Charla are at the front of my mind. Why can't I fuck Scarlett?

I grab a tissue to remove any extra lube I have on my hand and grab for one other toy. Pulling out the thrusting blue vibrator, I turn it on and insert it between Scarlett's wet folds. She bucks hard against my desk.

And that's what I focus on for the next few minutes. Scarlett grinding against my desk in pure pleasure until she can't take it anymore and then I do it all over again.

9

CHARLA

What was I thinking going to the Red Society to see East? It was completely stupid of me. Of course, he has other women. Women who obviously have no shame in performing sexual acts in front of other people. I try to shake the thoughts of that woman's mouth around his cock. I could never do something so reckless.

The deep purple towel drops to the floor as I wrap myself into my white silky robe. I don't even bother picking it up. For once I choose to not be perfect.

I'm sick of being perfect.

I'm sick of being my father's puppet.

Sliding my feet into my Jessica Simpson slippers, I leave the bathroom and head to my walk-in. I head for the far corner dresser and open the mahogany drawer. I grab what I need and head back out to my bed.

I need a release.

Once I'm settled on the bed, I let my robe fall away. I refuse to picture him as I position the vibrator at my entrance.

I will not picture him.

The minute I turn it on, his eyes appear in my mind. I hate myself for allowing him to cloud my thoughts. Suddenly, visions of the woman on her knees come into view. Getting off to her on her knees with East's cock in her mouth makes me feel dirty. Her saliva glistened on his cock. Remembering her tits nearly bouncing out of her red top as her mouth moved up and down. My toes start to curl as I bring myself to the brink of an orgasm. I shouldn't picture them. Not while I'm about to—

A pounding at my door startles me. Who on earth would be knocking at my door at this hour? The pounding continues with no signs of stopping.

Huffing in frustration, I throw my robe back on, not bothering to tie it, and head to see who is at my door, leaving my vibrator behind.

I take one look through my peephole and regret it instantly.

Why the hell is he here?

I open the door an inch. "Can I help you?" Annoyance laced in my voice. East better have a good reason for being here at this hour.

"Let me in, Charla."

Is he on crack? He has to be.

"I don't think so. What do you need?"

"We need to talk, right now."

"I think the night's early events did all the talking for you."

I go to shut the door, but he shoves his black boot between it and the door jam. The fucker.

"Charla," he warns. "I'll stand out here all night, knock-ing. I suggest you let me in."

I picture him for a moment, knocking repeatedly,

pissing off everyone else on this floor. "Fine," I huff and stand back to allow him to come in.

The minute he steps through the door, he shuts it, locking it. I laugh and shake my head. I don't know what this man is thinking. He isn't staying here long.

East eyes me. Taking me in from head to toe. Those dark eyes pause below my stomach. My robe isn't tied, exposing a little bit of skin as I hold it in place. It shouldn't make me feel alive, but the tic in his jaw as he stares at me does just that.

I clear my throat to gain his attention back to me. When his eyes flick to mine, I'm surprised to see the desire in them. It awakens my own desire and then I remember where he was prior to coming here.

"What can I do for you, East?"

"I can think of a few things." He smirks.

"What a scum thing to say. Please, go back to the chick in your office. I don't want to see you." I refuse to entertain his thoughts. Even if my body is dying to be touched by him.

"Let me make one thing clear. I am far from scum. Understand. Now, why did you come to my office?"

Looking back, I'm not sure why I came to his office. I had gotten off the phone with my father and the thoughts of being forced into marriage had me going to where I was hoping I could forget about being Ms. Perfect for a while. Boy, did I get more than I planned.

"I'm waiting for an answer."

"I, I don't know."

"Bullshit. Why did you come?"

I shrug. "I wanted to forget about life for a little bit and figured you might be able to help with that. But you were already preoccupied. End of story."

I go to unlock the door, but his hand stops me.

"We're not finished."

"I think we are."

"I said we're not finished."

East takes a step toward me. On instinct, I take a step back. Maybe it's the tattoos and his lip piercing that intimidate me.

"You need to leave, East."

"No one barges into my office without knocking and then slaps me across the face. Not without repercussions."

"That chick had your dick down her throat, and you wanted me to sit back and watch. I don't think so."

"Why the fuck did you barge in?" East's voice grows angry, causing me to flinch a little.

"I didn't mean to barge in, I was upset and when the man told me you were expecting me, I just assumed you knew I was coming."

East tilts his head, rubbing his chin, digesting my words. He is still angry. "Who told you I was expecting you because I was not expecting you. I certainly wouldn't have brought you up to my office, not while..." He stops, not finishing his sentence.

"A big guy, shaved head. I don't know, I didn't pay him much attention."

He shakes his head and takes a step closer. I back up until my back hits the wall. A smirk slowly grows across his face. It makes me want to slap him all over again. How dare he come here and then corner me. My body, on the other hand, wants him to corner me.

"Tsk tsk, nowhere to go." East comes close, putting his hands on his hips as he shakes his head at me. His cold words do nothing but agitate me further while I press my thighs together.

I don't back down though and for some odd reason, when I'm around him I feel brave. I can handle whatever he throws at me. I think.

Holding my head high, I straighten and look him in the eye. "I think it is time you leave, Mr. Sinclair."

"I'm pretty sure we got past the formal talk the minute I put my dick in your cunt. Don't you think?" He raises his eyebrows.

That asshole.

East Sinclair is an asshole.

Before I realize what's happening, his hand cups me hard between my thighs. Gasping, I'm not sure if it's because I'm shocked or if it's because of the electricity his hand sends through me. Can he feel how wet I am?

With his mouth inches from mine now, I can feel his minty breath. I almost want to lean and kiss him, but fear how he would respond so I don't.

"East," I whisper.

"What in your perfect life has you running into my arms now?" His lips are still inches from mine while his hand rubs up and down my arm. The other is still firmly in place. I can practically feel his fingers through the thin material of the robe. He has no clue I have nothing on underneath, or maybe he does. I don't know.

I swallow, at a loss for words.

East trails his nose across my cheek, moving to the crook of my neck where he bites me.

Hard.

I scream out, "Fuck, East!" I try to jerk away but his teeth are still on my skin and it hurts in the best possible way.

"I told you that I'm not what you want or need. Yet, you can't seem to stay away." He starts to rub a finger through my robe. I'm almost embarrassed because I'm wet and I'm certain he can tell now. Between what I was doing before he showed up and the effect he has on my body, there's no denying.

East lets go of my neck and steps back. He takes in my body again. I hate him. I hate how his eyes on me make me feel alive. He touches my robe, rubbing the silk between his fingers before pulling it from my grasp, exposing me.

I try to pull it back but he's fast and grabs my wrist, shaking his head. It should scare me, he should make me feel the same way Corey does when he touches me against my will.

Yet it doesn't it.

Maybe it's because deep down, I want East's hands on me. I'll take those strong hands anyway I can get them. Maybe it's because he helps me forget. I don't know, but what I do know is that he makes me feel the opposite of what Corey makes me feel and that should scare me.

It should definitely scare me.

10

CHARLA

East's eyes are filled with hot desire. The tic in his jaw turns me on further.

He wants me.

I should let him have me because who knows if I'll get this opportunity again. Especially with my father planning my life. Maybe I can lie to my father and tell him I'm dating someone. An idea comes to mind. What if East acts as my stand-in boyfriend? Just long enough to get my father off my ass.

My thoughts are interrupted the second East reaches out and pinches my nipple. I cry out from the initial pain.

"You make my dick hard, Charla. I think it's time I punish you." His deep voice is stern. Not a trace of humor. Once again, I should fear him; instead though, I am dying to be touched by him. I am curious to know just how he plans to punish me.

I decide to taunt him. "Punish me."

East stands there, in shock, I think. He wasn't expecting me to respond in such a way. I pull my wrist free and saunter back to my room. He can fuck me there. Hell, he can even tie me to my bedpost if he wants.

I feel his eyes on me as I make my way into my room. I stop short when I see the pink object on my bed. How could I forget what I was doing prior to East knocking on my door?

Embarrassment floods me. I turn quickly to bring us back out of the room but it's too late. His eyes are on one thing and one thing only.

My vibrator.

"What's this?"

"It's not what you— "

"Oh, I think it is. Were you touching yourself? After you left my club?"

I shake my head, words don't come. This is humiliating. I've never been caught like this before. Sure, Spence and I have discussed it, but he's my best friend. So not the same thing as this.

"Don't deny it. Your toy is out. You were either plea-suring yourself or about to pleasure yourself to what you witnessed in my office."

Oh my god.

My cheeks are probably six shades of red now. He's so blunt and brutal. I hate it.

He's not wrong though. That's the worst part. He's not wrong at all.

"That's what I thought," East smirks as he comes up closer to me. "Get on the bed. I want you on all fours."

"Wha— what?"

"Hands and knees now. Face the headboard." He grabs himself through his slacks as he makes his demands.

Demands I stupidly follow.

With my robe still on I climb onto my bed. Nervous

energy fills my body. I want his fingers on me again. I want him to fuck me the same way he did the night I begged him to.

East walks over to the side of the bed and picks up my vibrator, examining it.

"Do you enjoy pleasuring yourself?"

I close my eyes, unable to look at him. I can't. And the reality is, I only need one thing from him right now. And that's in his pants.

Just fuck me already and leave.

"If you are going to fuck me, can we get on with it? I have things to do."

"You have things to do late at night? Such as?" He pauses for a second. "Nothing unless it involves this toy in your cunt. That's the only thing you have going on."

"I hate you," I spit back. And I do. I may enjoy his cock, but I do not like him. Not at all.

"Hate is such a vile word coming from you, the prim and proper daughter of a politician."

I just shake my head. Why is he like this? Was he not raised better? Of course not, he owns a strip club. A buzzing sound causes me to freeze. He didn't.

Oh, but he did.

East comes up on his knees behind me on the bed and I want to turn to make sure his shoes are not on my bed, but all thoughts go out the window as soon as he touches my vibrator against my inner thigh.

"Tell me, Charla, have you ever let anyone else pleasure you with anything? A vibrator, dildo?" He rubs my toy against my sensitive skin, teasing me. It takes everything to not grind in response. I'm so pent up and desperate for a release, yet I refuse to give in easily to his game.

He grips my hip with one hand, pulling me back some,

before moving it to push my upper back down closer to the bed. My ass is now up in the air, for his viewing pleasure, I'm sure. I almost feel vulnerable on display like this. Then I remind myself of the business East owns. I'm sure he has had plenty of women on display.

He teases the vibrator against my wet folds before finally inserting it. I try to keep from moaning out, but it's no use. He slowly pulls it back before thrusting it back in hard. Over and over while the clit stimulator barely brushes my bud. He's rough. I like it though. Slow and hard thrusts have me panting and soaked, I can feel it dripping out of me.

I'm on the verge of exploding when he pulls my toy almost all the way out. "East." My voice is heavy. I need him to make me come and I need it to be now. The vibration against my clit causes my legs to shake. I hear the faint sound of a zipper, but I'm too consumed with agonizing pleasure to care.

"This is only the beginning of your punishment, Charla."

What?

A hand comes down hard on my ass at the same time he thrusts the vibrator back into me, causing me to explode. My entire body shakes as waves of pleasure overtake me. East slaps my ass several more times. Each time I moan or maybe scream out, I can't be too certain.

The only thing I'm certain of is the fact that I need East to fuck me and I need him to fuck me now.

11

EAST

Fuck, my dick is throbbing. I can't wait to sink into Charla's wet pussy. She's fucking dripping with desire. I want to taste her so damn bad, yet I refrain. Tonight, I'm punishing her. In return, I'm torturing myself, even if I want to lap up every last drop of her juices that currently run down her thigh.

I make quick work of getting the condom on before slapping her ass cheek again. It's already red from the last few slaps. I don't give a fuck though. She's going to learn a lesson.

No one slaps me and gets away with it.

No one.

I line my cock up fast, not giving her any time to process before I slam into her cunt. I dig my fingers into her hips as I pull back ever so slowly. It's agony for both of us. I know she wants more because of the whimper that leaves her mouth when I pulled back. I slam in hard again, before repeating the slow motion of pulling back. Just like with her pink vibrator, I tease her over and over, her pussy growing wet all over again.

God, she feels so good. I drive into her over and over and every so often I slap her ass. I know she's getting close because she keeps begging me to let her come. Too bad I'm an asshole and won't let her have her orgasm yet. She'll get it when I'm good and ready for her to have it.

I pull almost all the way out and stop.

"East, please." Charla turns to look at me. The hunger she has for my dick is written across her face, but there's something else. I can't put my finger on it so instead I push her neck causing her upper body down further on the bed. That's right, raise that pretty little cunt up higher for me.

Taking a finger, I run it along her soaked folds. Once it's good and wet, I slide it into her, knowing full well it's not what she wants. She surprises me, though, as she pushes her ass up more.

"Good girl."

Removing my finger, I thrust my dick back into her and nearly blow my load right there. She feels too good. It's never felt this good. I quickly shove that thought to the back of my mind while I drive into her, picking up my pace. My grip on her hips will leave her bruised. I have a feeling she won't mind though. She likes the pain I give her.

Without warning, her pussy clamps down around my cock as she screams out.

Fuck.

My own release comes on fast. I fucking unload inside of her harder than I ever have in my life, all the while squeezing her silky skin. Yup, she'll have marks for sure now.

I pull out and Charla collapses on the bed.

"Lock the bottom lock on your way out." Her breathless words leave her mouth in barely more than a whisper, yet I hear them loud and clear.

Jesus.

———

I saw myself out of Charla's condo a week ago, yet somehow it feels like last night. I can picture it all so vividly. Her red ass, her perfect cunt. I can hear her moans and cries clear as day.

Why though?

No woman clouds my thoughts, no pussy stays on my mind. Call me a selfish prick, I am who I am, and Charla Krauss should be no different.

I continue running on the treadmill wishing like hell the rain would stop. Running outside is so much better. I can clear my thoughts and refocus. I can't do that on this piece of equipment, which is why I hate the dreadmill.

Frustrated, I slam my hand down on the stop button. I need another way to clear my head. I could contact Scarlett, except I know fucking her won't clear my head. Not while I'm stuck on Charla anyway.

Taking my towel, I wipe the sweat from my face and pull out my phone. I felt it vibrate earlier and chose to ignore it. A number I don't recognize flashes on my lock screen. Swiping to unlock my phone, I open the text message.

It's Charla, I have a proposition for you.

A proposition for me? Why? I don't do favors for people. I'm a businessman. A damn good businessman. I type out a quick response. Charla is the last thing I need on my fucking mind as is.

Not interested

At least hear me out first.

No

I'm desperate. Can we meet & talk over dinner?

Charla, a desperate woman? I find that hard to believe. She has Daddy's money and an expensive pad. She's not desperate.

Desperate doesn't look good on a woman. You know that, right?

Yes, asshole. I just need you to pretend to

be my boyfriend. Until my father gets off
my case.

Well, well, this is interesting. She wants me to pretend to date her so dearest daddy gets off her ass. Shocker. However, I'm intrigued.

Dinner at The Vine 7pm do not be late

I'm never late. See you soon, oh and East.
Thank you.

Great, now she's thanking me, and I haven't even agreed to whatever shit she is trying to drag me into. I really shouldn't entertain her and her drama. She is in over her head and has allowed people to control her for far too long. She cares more about her perfect image than she does her freedom and that's just sad. I see it daily. I wasn't lying to her when I told her I see women stuck.

Scarlett comes to mind. Her mother dragged her into a world of stripping. Scarlett wanted nothing to do with it. Hated it, hated me.

Until she didn't.

See, dancing and taking off clothes pay her bills. Bills that her mother neglected to pay. Alcohol was a priority.

Still is. It wasn't always that way. Her mother was a stripper for my grandfather and then she fell pregnant. She hooked up with a regular and he wanted nothing to do with her. Who knows the real story? That is just one of the rumors I've heard over the years. The only thing I know for sure is that she did work here for a long time before Scarlett was old enough to take over her spot. *Young with perky tits* were her mother's exact words. I'll never forget sitting across from my grandfather when Rochelle came in to offer up Scarlett.

What kind of parent does that to their child?

12

East hasn't arrived yet. The hostess seated me in a back corner before handing me a menu. I'm early. *I'm always early.*

It's the way I was taught. My father never stood for tardiness and therefore I was conditioned to be at least fifteen minutes early to wherever it was I needed to be. I mean, it's a good habit to get into it. Especially at work. Not that I've ever been late to work.

I've never been late to work.

I guess Daddy's conditioning wasn't all that terrible. Except now I am starting to hate it. I hate everything about what's happening in my life and how I feel like I have no control. I just don't know how to break the cycle. I don't know how to get my father to see Corey is all wrong for me.

That's why I sit here now, waiting on the man covered in tattoos who scares me so good. The one makes my body come alive in ways it never has before. It's why I'm hoping my low-cut top and tight dress pants distract East enough that he'll say yes. I need him to say yes to my wild plan. It's the only plan I have and I need it to work. It has to.

Or else.

I spot East walking toward me, the hostess right next to him. Her eyes bore into him. Yeah, hunny, he does look that good. He looks good. Damn good. His eyes find mine and he never looks away, not while he pulls out his chair. Not while the hostess sets down his menu. Not while the hostess asks if there's anything she can get him. It makes my stomach flutter.

I kind of like it.

I have his attention and she doesn't. She glares at me quickly before flashing me a fake smile and walking away. Please, I know all about fake smiles. I am the queen of fake smiles. It has zero effect on me. Once upon a time, I would have been offended by her actions. I no longer care. I don't want to be that person anymore. She takes our drink order and saunters off, clearly still trying to get East's attention.

"Why do I need to be your stand-in, Charla?"

I swallow. "My father wants me to marry Corey." I cringe. I can't even stand to say the words.

"Not my problem. Tell him no. You are an adult."

"He won't hear it." I shake my head. "I tried. I told him I didn't want to marry him. I've even been avoiding him for over a week now because he wants to hold a dinner to make Corey and I official."

"Again, not my problem," East says as he waves the waiter over.

A young man, probably twenty-one, with blonde hair and bright blue eyes walks returns with our drink orders. He flashes me a smile followed by a wink. For a few seconds, I allow myself to get lost in his eyes. I'm flattered, but he doesn't give me the same vibes that East gives.

"Eyes on me." A stern voice pops my bubble. "I'll have the filet mignon. Charla, what would you like?"

Shock must be evident on my face as East looks at me with a pointed stare. He just snapped at our server. What in the hell? But also, I'm allowed to order my own meal? That's rare. It's almost refreshing. He clears his throat, clearly waiting on me.

I glance at the menu, but it's a blur. So many confusing thoughts run rampant right now in my mind.

"Uh, I will have the same as him." I nod toward East, who shakes his head and chuckles quietly.

As soon as the server walks away, I dive back into my desperate plea. "Come on, East. It isn't like we are we really dating. It's just a front until my father gets over Corey." My throat is dry. I quickly take a sip of my water The minute it hits my lips, I start to relax some. East must agree. I'm prepared to do anything. Well, almost anything.

Glancing at him with the glass still at my lips, I wink. His uninterested expression falters, but only for a second.

"Charla, I still don't see how I can be of help. You need to just speak up to your father."

I ponder his words. "I've already tried to. Daddy is dead set on this arrangement."

"Look, you're a grown woman. You make your own money. What are you concerned about? Not pleasing him?"

I open my mouth to respond but catch East's hands that are laid out on the table in front of him, balled into fists. His veins thick. Who knew that could be hot? My eyes dart to his face, his hard expression stares off into the distance. I turn to see what has his attention.

Oh my god.

No.

I turn back to face East. His eyes are still trained on him. *Please don't let him come this way.*

Please, God.

Wait, was that a woman on his arm? I didn't pay enough attention as panic hit. I don't care, just please don't come this way.

East swallows thickly and nods his head slightly.

No, no, no.

I can practically feel his slimy eyes boring into the back of my head. Thinking quickly, I place my hands on top of East's fists that are still balled up. He tenses. Our eyes connect and I silently beg him to go along with my wild idea. *Please, East.* I need him too.

Now.

"Well, what do we have here?" Corey's disgusting voice sounds from behind me as he walks up to our table. I internally cringe and keep a firm grip on East. My French manicure looks strange against his skin. East gives me a look before acknowledging the man I'm meant to marry.

"Corey, I'd say it's a pleasure to see you, except it's not."

Holy shit.

East opens his hands slowly and entwines his fingers through mine. It's a shock, but boy do his hands feel good in mine.

Corey gives no response to East as he studies our hands before addressing me. "What's this, Charla? Out with another man?"

"I am." I finally look at the scum and hold my head high. Sure enough, there's a chick standing next to him. She's a blonde, beautiful too, but as fake as they come. Her pink lipstick is smudged a little. That means... my eyes trail back to Corey. His dress shirt is a little loose and wrinkled a good bit. Upon closer inspection, I see it. The faint lipstick stains on his collar.

What a sleazeball.

"Does your father know about this?" He waves between

East and me.

"Does my father know about you and her?" I quip in return. "Or should I take a photo and send it to him?"

Corey huffs, anger evident that I spoke to him in such a manner. "You know your father will never approve of this filth, all covered in tattoos with an earring in his lip."

"What I have on my body has nothing to do with what kind of man I am. I can guarantee I'm more man than you'll ever be."

Hot damn.

My eyes go to the man across from me. His jaw is set, eyes on Corey. Even with an annoyed expression on his face, he looks hot.

"Charla, I think it's time you go home before I let your father know about this."

"I'm not five— "

East interrupts me. "Charla is a grown woman, fully capable of making her own decisions." He practically growls the words as his teeth grind.

He's not wrong. Even if choosing to associate with him turns out to be a bad idea, it's my choice. One I'm making.

"She's going to tarnish my reputation by being with you. I won't have it."

I whip my head back toward Corey. Now I'm pissed. I pull out of East's grip and stand. I get right in Corey's face. "Lucky for me, your reputation isn't my fucking problem. As a matter of fact, I'm certain your career would be over if I spoke of the things you have done to me."

"Charla," Corey warns, but I hold my hand up to silence him. I'm not finished.

"Don't Charla me, I've had enough of your shit. It ends now. You need to leave."

The blonde mumbles something in his ear as the server

walks up with our food.

Perfect timing.

"Umm, is everything okay? Should I get my manager?" Poor guy looks between all of us as he sets our food down.

"Yes—"

"No." Corey interrupts me before I can finish.

Our waiter rushes away without another word, and I can only hope that he is going to get a manager before this escalates further.

"I believe Charla asked you to leave. I would respect her wishes unless you want the press to pry into what kind of man you truly are. One who demands to marry one woman while out with another, lipstick stains and all."

My head whips in East's direction. What he just said rings loud and clear. Corey is vile. He is not the man for me.

"You need to leave, Corey—"

"Sir, I'm going to have to ask you to leave." An older gentleman, much older than me, walks up to our table. The manager, I assume.

Corey straightens. "This isn't over," he growls as he pushes past me. East stands abruptly, and I have to put my hand on his chest to prevent him from going after the piece of shit.

"He's not worth it, East. Let's sit back down and eat."

The tic in his jaw tells me he's not ready to let Corey pushing me go. Without thinking, I lean up and kiss his jaw. He smells divine. I'd like to do more than place a kiss on him, but East Sinclair doesn't do more.

His eyes soften slightly before he steps back and takes his seat.

Thank goodness. I look around as I return to my seat. It's then that I see many eyes on us.

Shit.

13

CHARLA

Pounding comes from the front door. I groan as I get out of bed and head toward the annoying sound. Whoever it is doesn't let up as they continue pounding.

After dinner with East, I went home. I called Spencer and opened a bottle of pink Moscato. He came over and we drank the rest of the night away. Now here I am with a slight headache and someone at my door.

"I'm coming!" I finally shout as I make my way to the entrance. I open the door without looking through the peephole and to my utter surprise, my father is standing in front of me.

Crap.

"Good morning, Charla."

"Hi, Daddy." I try to sound cheerful, though I am anything but.

He walks straight past me and goes to the living room.

"I wasn't expecting you," I state as I watch him walk right up to the windows that East had me pressed up against not too long ago. My father stares out at the ocean and says nothing. That makes me nervous.

"Daddy?"

"Your behavior recently is a disappointment. I expect better of you."

I stare at him even though he can't see me. My behavior? He can't be serious. I see movement from the corner of my eye. Spencer. He's still here? Maybe he crashed here. I don't remember. He stands in the shadows of my hall, hands on his hips. The look on his face tells me he isn't happy with what my father just said. I should speak up. I need to. It's just in person with daddy is scary.

"Charla, did you hear me?"

Right, my father is expecting me to respond.

"Sorry, Daddy, I was..." I pause trying to find the words. However, before I can come up with the right words my father lashes out.

"You were what? Thinking of that punk of a business owner?"

"What?" Shock is evident in my voice.

"A man that owns a strip joint, one that allows women to take their clothes off for a dollar, isn't a man at all. Remember, Charla, your mother left you, us, to be a stripper." He turns to look at me. "I don't want you associating with that guy anymore. It will do nothing but make us look bad. I don't need our image ruined for some punk."

Image. Right. It's always about image.

Something I'm so sick of hearing. I'm sick of caring about what others think. Shaking my head, I try to gather my thoughts.

"Charla, are you listening to me?" My father's voice tells me he is now angry.

Great.

"I am."

"Good, you know I don't like having to repeat myself."

He scolds me as if I'm still a child. It pisses me off and I have to hold my tongue to keep from saying something I'll most likely regret.

"Tomorrow evening is set. I've arranged a dinner for Corey and you. You will apologize for your behavior, and he will propose."

What in the hell?

Something snaps inside of my soul.

"No."

"What did you just say to me?"

It's now or never. I swallow my fear and lift my chin to meet his gaze. "I said no. No, I will not be going to dinner with Corey. I will not be apologizing, and I certainly will not be getting engaged to that creep."

"Excuse me?" The fury in his voice should scare me right into submission, but I refuse.

"I will not attend anything that involves Corey. He's violent and he has a different woman weekly. No, thank you."

Holy shit! I actually did it. Spoke up. Fear still cripples me, I look down at my hands, they are shaking. When I look back at my father, I see just how angry he is. His face is beat red.

"Charla Ann! What has gotten into you?"

"Daddy, Corey has put bruises on me. He's tried to force himself on me. I won't have it, and you shouldn't want that for me."

"Don't be silly. He told me about your arm."

"He did?"

"Of course. What else was he supposed to do to prevent you from being with that punk?"

Rage fills me.

"That's not what happened! Seriously, that's what Corey told you?" I shake my head, hands ball into my fist at my sides. Nope, no way. This ends now.

"Calm down, Corey would not lie to me."

I laugh. I can't believe Corey. "Oh, but he did because Corey was in my face fighting with me and grabbed me to prevent me from leaving him. Mr. Sinclair, or should I say the punk, happened to be walking past and saw the entire thing."

"Now, Charla."

"No, Daddy! Don't Charla me. Corey was hurting me. This has happened more than once. I'm done. Do you hear me?" I'm now visibly shaking; all I see is red. How can my father not believe me? "Perhaps if Corey kept his nasty hands off of me, I wouldn't be seeing East now."

"Don't be ridiculous, you are not seeing that man. That stops today."

"I am and I will continue seeing him. There's nothing you can do to stop that. How about you believe your daughter for once?"

I all but shout at him. Spencer steps out from the shadows, causing us to both turn and look at him.

"Spencer." My father nods.

"Sir." Spence looks nervous. "What Charla is saying is true. Corey has pushed himself on her more than once."

"Enough, Spencer. This conversation is between Charla and myself. You should show yourself out."

With my mouth gaping, I look at my best friend. He nods.

"I'll call you later, Charla. Mr. Krauss, for what it's worth, Mr. Sinclair has been nothing but a gentleman to your daughter. He treats her better than Corey ever has. Ever will."

Spencer walks out without looking back, leaving me standing alone with my father. I'm frustrated. This entire situation could have been avoided if my father would just stop with his demands. I turn and look at the man who raised me.

"I will not be seeing Corey, end of discussion. Now if you'll excuse me, I would like to shower. I have things to do today."

Anger and arrogance roll off of my father's movements as he walks past me. When he gets to the foyer, he stops with his hand on the knob.

"I expect you at dinner tomorrow. Details will be emailed. Oh, and Charla." He pauses and a sinister smile forms across his face. "Remember who pays for this suite."

He walks out, shutting the door, effectively ending the conversation.

That asshole.

I've never called my father that before, but right now, that's what he is. An asshole, plain and simple.

I text Spencer and head for my bathroom. I start the shower and walk in, still in my clothes.

Spencer emerges minutes later. "Charla, are you okay?"

I nod, afraid that if I speak, tears will come. I don't want to cry. How can a girl who has everything feel so trapped?

Spencer pulls me from under the spray of water and hugs me tightly. He holds me and allows me to finally breakdown.

And that's exactly what I do. I let go and cry.

My life is a mess and yet all I want right now is East, the bad boy who makes me forget about my perfectly imperfect life.

14

Dinner with my father is supposed to be in thirty minutes. I'm not there.

Instead, I'm sitting in the parking lot of The Red Society. Trying to find the courage to go in is like trying to stand up to my father.

It's hard.

And while I already know there will be hell to pay for not showing, I'm okay with that. At least for now.

My mind drifts to East. How his hands felt on my body. Strong hands that grasped me tightly. A cock that felt way better than any before him. I'd be lying if I said I hadn't thought of our encounter daily, while at work, taking a shower, while getting ready.

Let's face it, I want more of East Sinclair, the cold man who does carnal things to my body. Things I happened to enjoy. Things I should probably be ashamed about. But I'm not.

My phone dings, I have a message. Probably Daddy asking where I am.

Leaning over to the passenger seat to retrieve my phone

from my handbag that sits on the floorboard, I think of what to reply with. What excuse I can make? However, when I sit up a scream rips through me and I drop my phone.

Standing in front of my car dressed in all black, is darkness himself. East walks to my side of the car and I lower the window, flashing him a nervous smile.

"Why are you here?" Annoyance oozes from him.

That's not the vibe I was hoping for. "I um... I was kind of hoping to see you."

"We both know that's not a good idea, Charla."

"I'm not here for good ideas. In fact, I'm sick of good ideas."

East's eyes narrow for a few seconds. He makes me nervous, or maybe it's the butterflies that seem to take flight whenever he's nearby. I don't know.

"Get out of the car."

"Huh?"

"Get. Out. Of. The. Car. Now."

"So demanding," I tease as I unbuckle and open the door, slowly stepping out.

He's on me fast. His lips nip hard at my neck. It shocks me at first. I wasn't expecting him to come at me. Suddenly I remember we are in the parking lot and that someone could see me. See us.

I pull back quickly and glance around to find no one around. It's desolated here, dark.

"What's wrong? Afraid to be seen with me? I told you I'm not a good idea." East's husky voice brings me back to looking directly at him.

"I told you, I like bad ideas."

"You don't know what you are talking about, silly girl."

My phone rings. Shit. There's a ninety-nine percent chance that it is my father.

"Are you going to answer that?"

I shake my head and reach in the car for my phone so I can silence it. "I don't want to talk to whoever is calling."

"Is that so?"

East steps closer to me and grabs my chin. He looks like he wants to say something but before he can, my phone starts up again, vibrating in my hand. I glance and see Corey's name. East sees it too.

Now if I was a smart girl, I would have just ignored the call. But no. I do the complete opposite. I answer.

"What, Corey?"

"Where are you? You're late." Pure annoyance is laced in his voice. I don't care though. He's not entitled to know my whereabouts.

"I'm not coming. I told my father that. Sorry if you didn't get the memo."

Yes, I know I'm poking the bear, I'm fed up.

"What do you mean you're not coming? Your father requires your presence. I require it."

I snort. "You? You don't get to require anything of me. Now if you'll excuse me, I need to get back to my date." I wink at East, who looks pretty angry.

"Date?! What the fuck, Charla! Who are you with?" Corey screams through the line.

"That's none of — "

East snatches the phone from my hand and ends the call.

"Hey!"

He says nothing as I watch him power down my phone and then toss it back onto my leather seat. He grabs the keys out of the ignition and slams my door quicker than I can process.

"What are you doing?"

His reaction should make me worry, yet it does the complete opposite. East makes me feel excited, alive.

He still says nothing as he pulls me along toward the entrance of his club. A place I know I don't belong. I resist a little as we come up to the doors.

"What? Now you're afraid?" He smirks.

"I… I don't… it's just not my scene."

"Fine, right here will do." He pushes me up against the building.

What? What's that supposed to mean?

"Do what?" He can't possibly mean sex. There's no way. Someone could walk up and see.

"Bad things," is the only response I get before his lips are on my neck, followed by him biting and sucking. And hell if it doesn't turn me on.

He's rough, but not careless. It feels good. So good. Too good.

My hands find his dark hair and instantly mess up his perfectly styled look. I don't give a shit either. If he can bite me, I can fuck up his hair.

East's hands roam my body. He hikes my leg up and bunches my red fitted dress in his hands, pulling it up. I'm not wearing anything under it. I should stop him from exposing me like this out here. I don't though, instead, I let my hands glide down his chest. I want to feel him.

He freezes at my touch and immediately steps back.

He looks me over. Something dark and sinister registers in his eyes when they land on my bare pussy that has been exposed.

East grabs my hands and places them above my head,

locking them in place with one of his strong hands. I don't even bother to fight him. Adrenaline courses through my veins. Why am I like this with him?

His stare penetrates me until he looks down at my chest. He takes his free hand and rubs a thumb over my nipple that's hardened beneath the thin red fabric. My body is begging to be touched by him. Begging to be bitten by him. To be claimed by him.

And while my body wants all those things, my mind is screaming to take this behind closed doors. Part of me finds this thrilling. Is this what it feels like to be alive? The other part of me, well I can picture it. Someone seeing me, a politician's daughter on public display with the strip club owner. The reporters would have a field day.

"East let's go somewhere... more private."

"Are you ashamed to be seen with me?" East asks as his hand cups me. He very slowly inserts a finger into my already wet flesh.

I can only moan in response. All common sense floats away as my head falls back against the concrete.

He continues teasing me while biting at my neck. I allow him to because he's bringing me to my new favorite high.

The high of East Sinclair.

He's bringing me to that place I've found that I love. His touch has me so close that my arms are fighting to be free. He is strong though and tightens his grip on me.

Suddenly, East stills, leaving his finger in me, unmoving.

"East," I groan in agony as I try to grind on his hand.

Fuck.

He presses his body against mine so I can't move.

However, I feel his erection and that right there has me wanting more. Now.

"Come on, East."

"Answer me, Charla. Are you ashamed to be seen with me? To have someone see you doing erotic things in public with me? Afraid it will tarnish your perfect image?"

"We're doing this right now?" He's so annoying. I try to move against him, to feel anything. But can't quite hit where I need to in order to lose myself. "East, shut up and just touch me."

My blunt words must have hit a nerve, his eyes darken before his lips curl up into a snarl. He bites along my jaw down to my neck. Again, he's rough and I know just by the way he nips and sucks that there will be marks I will be unable to hide tomorrow.

Oh well.

I like the fact that he is marking me.

As if he is making me his.

East distracts me as he begins to work his magic again. Almost instantly, I come apart at his touch. I moan out, not caring who can hear me or even see me now.

East wins this round.

15

EAST

The minute Charla clenches around my fingers, I know I've got her right where I want her. I'm going to fuck her right here against my fucking building, and I won't stop until she screams out my name.

In one quick move, I pull my fingers out of her and undo my belt and the button of my pants, pulling the zipper down allowing my erect dick to spring free. A little bit of precum pools at the tip, reminding me I don't have a condom. Swiping the substance with my thumb, I rub it against her lips. Shocking her at first. But then she darts her tongue out licking her lips.

"Tell me you are on birth control." Because I need to be inside of her right now. I know she has to be. She would be foolish not to be.

"I am but..."

I place my finger over her lips, rubbing what's left to silence her. Without another word, I line my cock up with her dripping pussy and push straight in, not even waiting for her to fight me on this.

And fuck me if she doesn't feel damn good.

Fuck.

This is a dangerous game to play, especially with someone like Charla. Her cunt feels incredible as it tightens around me. I won't last like this.

I pound into her hard, and I know the exterior wall must be scrapping across her bare skin, yet I don't stop. I know she likes pleasure mixed with pain, and for some reason, that thought drives me into her harder.

"East." She moans, enticing me further. My dick likes the way she calls out for me.

She tries to grab out for me and I grab her hands, bringing them back above her head. I don't do touching. No touching, no intimacy.

Just fucking.

That's the way I like it.

When she touches me, it causes me to feel too much and I don't need that bullshit in my life.

At least that is what I tell myself as I bite her nipple through her dress, causing her pussy to clench around me. It brings her over the edge just like I knew it would, and she fucking screams out my name. She screams it out over and over, causing me to fucking come inside her.

As soon as my dick stops jerking inside her perfect pussy, I pull out and tuck myself back into my pants and pull down her dress. Charla doesn't respond, just fixes her hair and smooths her dress.

"That was..."

"Dirty. That was dirty for you to do such a thing in public, right?"

"Um... well, yes."

"Go home."

Charla nods. She came here to get what she wanted and nothing more. She craves my dick. She craves the high. I should end it and not play into this game except my dick craves her too. It craves her wet pussy way more than I care to admit.

When she starts to head for her SUV, I call out, "Oh, and Charla?"

She glances over her shoulder at me.

"I'm enjoying watching you walk away with my cum dripping down your thighs."

Charla smirks. She has the nerve to smirk at me. "Too bad you are too far away to see such a sight." She winks and continues toward her car.

Her damn smart mouth. Just like that, my dick is hard again. I take long strides and pull her hair as soon as I can reach her, halting her moves. I pull her back against me and grab her pussy through her dress. The fabric instantly grows wet. A mixture of us both. Evidence of us.

"Such a smart mouth," I whisper to her ear before biting it lightly.

"Just stating the truth."

My cock twitches.

I urge her to her SUV and tell her to unlock the doors then I pull open the back door.

"Bend over."

"What?"

Without explaining, I push her down, arms under her stomach against the dark leather. Hiking her dress back up, I reach between her thighs and nudge them further apart.

Just feeling my cum on her has me losing my mind. The urgency to be back in her wet warmth has me losing control.

Yanking my pants down, I dive my cock straight inside of her. She's so wet there is no resistance. None at all.

And fuck me at the sound that leaves her lips.

I drive into her relentlessly and she takes it beautifully. So willing. I grab her blonde hair, pulling her head back toward me. Not enough to hurt her though. Or maybe it does. I don't care. I just know it sets her body on fire.

And set it afire do I.

Charla clenches and screams out my name. I knew she liked it rough. I fucking knew it.

"You like it hard, don't you? Like a dirty little slut."

"Yes... yes..."

Her admission strokes my ego. I wish it didn't, but it does. And when I pull a little harder, her pussy tightens, and her legs shake.

Charla screams out louder than she ever has before. It fucking drives me to fuck her harder. Her screams alone thrill me to new heights and before I know it, I'm blowing my load into her for the second time tonight.

Fucking Charla Krauss.

―――――――

I left Charla at her SUV last night without saying a word. After fucking Charla senseless right outside of my club, I had to get away. I needed space. I needed to focus on work and not wanting to fuck her again and again. So, I did what I do best, I focused on my business. I made sure everything was in order and running smoothly. Marc and Rian gave me a look more than once that said they knew, I just chose to ignore it.

Just like right now. I'm ignoring the ringing of my phone. I haven't answered or even bothered to look, yet I have a pretty good idea of who it is. Why? Because this is the third time in less than ten minutes that it's gone off.

Why can't she take a hint? I grumble but finally grab it and answer.

"Yes?"

"East?"

"You called me and you're going to question if it's me?"

"You don't have to be so rude." She huffs in annoyance. Good, now she knows how I feel.

"Look, I was hoping, I don't know, that maybe you'll attend an event with me."

"And why would I do that?"

"Because you're supposed to play the part of the guy I'm dating."

"Right. Look, I don't know if that's a good idea. I think you need to handle your own problems and leave me out of it. This is over." I pull the phone away to hang up but stop short when I hear her plea.

"Please, East. If I have to go alone--" Her desperate words get to me. If she has to go alone what?

"Go on."

"My father will force me to be with Corey. Please. I can't stand to be near him. I can't handle this on my own. Just please."

"You sound desperate begging. Why don't you just tell daddy dearest what Corey has done?"

"I have, he doesn't believe me."

What the fuck? What father doesn't believe his own daughter? A tightening feeling forms in my chest and against my better judgment, I agree.

"Fine, text me the details. But Charla—"

"I'll do whatever you want."

"Good girl."

I hang up with a smile on my face. She has no idea what she just agreed to.

16

CHARLA

At five-fifty-five, East rings for me. He sure doesn't like to be kept waiting. Like right now.

I swear the elevator is running slower than normal and it's stopping at what seems like every floor on the way down.

The second the doors open in the lobby I rush off, not caring about those around me.

I spot East immediately and holy fuck me. There he stands dressed in all black. I'm not even kidding. His suit is solid black. Black dress shirt under the blazer and a black bowtie to match. His black shoes are shined, not a scuff on them. Stepping up to him, I notice that even his cuff links are black. His dark hair is styled to sexy perfection, and he smells so damn good.

He resembles a fallen angel. And boy do I love what that angel does to my body.

"It's after six." He tsks as he points to his expensive watch on his wrist. That too is black. Most likely black titanium.

"It's only two minutes after and the elevator kept stopping on the way down."

East doesn't bother to respond. He never does. Instead, he places his hand on the small of my back and quickly guides us out to a waiting limo. Black with black rims. How? Why?

"Is this yours?"

"It is. Now get in."

Well, shit.

Once the driver pulls out, I relax a little. I had a sick feeling that he would not show for my father's event, but here we are, and he certainly didn't disappoint.

Daddy is going to be so angry. He will not cause a scene though, thankfully. He would never scold me or voice his distaste anywhere that the reporters lurk and they will certainly be lurking tonight too. The tabloids have had a bit of fun with my name lately. They have mentioned me not being next to Corey and have made their speculations. It's a joke really. A sick, sick joke that I no longer want to be a part of.

I sigh, for once grateful that Daddy must remain perfect.

Perfect is overrated.

I need to think of something else, I don't want to keep focusing on my image.

"So, East, why the limo for just the two of us?"

He looks at me, there's a twinkle in his dark eyes. I catch the shimmer of his lip ring as a devilish grin appears across his face. It should worry me. Honestly it should do more than worry me. Something must be wrong with me because he looks like he wants to eat me alive and that alone turns me on. It gets my blood flowing and I have to clench my thighs.

"I have plans later."

My heart sinks. "Oh." I'm assuming after he gets rid of me, he'll be out on the town with others. Good to know. As much as it should not bother me, it does.

"What's wrong, Charla?"

"Nothing, I— "

"Save it. Remember I don't do bullshit."

I roll my eyes and turn to look out the window. The city lights are a blur as we speed past, continuing on our way.

Tonight's event is being held at Daddy's show house. The charity event is always held here each year. It wouldn't shock me if it was purchased just for this event.

I shake my head in disgust and run my hands over my thighs, smoothing my dress. The silver fabric hugs my body perfectly, just like all my gowns. It begins to flow out at my lower legs and continues flowing down into a short train. My pink stilettos are barely noticeable when I walk. Just a pop of color.

A hand suddenly grips my jaw, startling me. I'm forced to meet East's dark eyes. His hard stare causes my heart rate to spike.

"The limo is for us after we leave your father's event."

"Wha..what?"

"Don't look so confused. Remember when you said you'll do whatever I want as long as I attend this thing?"

I nod. I did, after all agree to do whatever he wanted.

"Good, because I plan to fuck you all over this limo." He releases his grip on me and sits back, adjusting the hard-on that he very clearly has.

Hot damn.

I'm left speechless.

I'm not sure how we make it to my father's with minutes to spare, yet we do.

As the car is put in park, East leans over to me, his hot breath against my ears sends shivers down my spine.

"Let's get this over with so I can devour you." He leans back and gently touches me, closing my mouth that damn sure hit the ground with his blunt words.

The driver opens our door then, effectively ending the moment. East climbs out first then holds his hand out for me to take. I do so willingly, almost certain that there is at least one reporter with a camera guy standing out here.

I step out and sure enough, there's a camera on us, snapping away. I smile at East. He just nods and places his hand on my back, nearly digging into my skin.

"Leeches. They are like leeches, always trying to suck on whatever gossip they can find."

He's not exactly wrong. "I've never thought of it that way, but you're correct."

"It's why I prefer to stay out of the flashing lights. I've had enough of people in my business to last a lifetime."

His honesty hits a nerve. He couldn't be more right. I've always had cameras in my face. I used to live for those shining moments. But now, I'd give anything for them to dim and burn out.

I am, however, curious as to why he's had the reporters in his life. Surely it couldn't be because of his strip club? That would have fizzled out fast. I decide to test the waters.

"What do you mean you've had enough people in your business to last a lifetime?"

He gives me a sideways glance and shakes his head.

"Come on, tell me."

"Drop it, Charla." His lips press into a thin line. He's not going to tell me. Not tonight anyway.

"Charla!" Spencer's voice is one I welcome.

"Hey, Spence!" I pull my best friend in for a hug. He tightly hugs me in return, not letting me go.

"I see you really did bring him. You are going to be on the chopping block tomorrow, you realize that, right?"

I laugh as I step back, East immediately snakes his hand around my waist, gripping me so hard I nearly wince. Spencer doesn't miss it either.

His voice is quiet when he speaks. "I hope you are treating her right because this," he discreetly points a finger between us, "is going to cause Charla a lot of problems."

"It'll be fine." I swallow, not liking the way my voice sounds.

East gives me a tight squeeze before releasing me. He holds his hand out for Spencer to shake. I'm just as confused as Spencer, but he reaches out and shakes his hand in return. East doesn't release it, instead, he stares at their joined hands for a few before looking up at my friend.

"There's no doubt that I am treating Ms. Krauss right. Don't ever think differently. I am not like most of the scum that is walking around this room right now. Charla asked me to attend with her, if she has problems, it's only because she chose to have them." With that, East releases Spencer's hand.

Spencer glances at me for a second and shakes his head before turning his attention back to the devil that stands next to me.

"Understood. Just wanted to make sure you are aware."

I don't doubt for a second that there will be hell to pay for this stunt. Not for a second. It's just I can't play the part my father wants me to play, and I need him to see that. I'm done caving just to please my father.

"Charla, this will result in an absolute shit show."

"I know." I reach out and squeeze Spencer's arm, hoping to reassure him.

"Excuse me, I need a drink."

I nod as I watch my friend turn and disappear into the crowd of people. People that ooze wealth with their designer suits and gowns. I feel eyes on me and not in a good kind of feeling way. I look around and spot my father standing at the far end of the room. He is staring directly at us. He is pissed off.

His expression alone confirms that tonight will be a shit show. No doubt about it.

17

CHARLA

Squeezing East's hand, I swallow down all the anxiety I feel.

"Come on, let's break the ice."

"Remember, you are a grown woman. Act like it and don't take any shit."

His words are harsh, yet they speak truth. I am an adult and my father cannot keep controlling me like this. Fingers crossed that he understands that tonight and going forward.

"Mr. Krauss, it's good to see you again." East wastes no time sticking his hand out to shake my father's hand. And if on cue, my father shakes his, a fake smile in place.

"Let's not sugar coat." My father releases East's hand and pulls me in, kissing each cheek. "We've talked about this, Charla. Why must you defy me?"

"It's good to see you too." Sarcasm drips from my mouth. He's brazen, acting like this in such a public setting.

"I think it's best your friend should see himself out before Corey sees you with him."

"I don't care if Corey sees me with someone. I am not Corey's girlfriend."

"No, you are to be his fiancé and this will have the reporters ripping us apart due to your actions. Now please show your friend out."

"His name is Eas— "

"It's Mr. Sinclair. Did you know that I am the largest donor of the evening? How do you think it would look if I left early? Of course, I could stop and let the tabloids know that Mr. Krauss himself asked me to leave and that I was not welcomed even though I have given such a generous amount in support of helping underprivileged children."

Holy mother of God.

East didn't tell me he was donating to tonight's event. I had no idea. And to be the largest donor? Hell, he never fails to impress me. It almost makes my heart swell.

Fury flares in my father's eyes. I'm not sure I've ever seen him so angry. I can't help but chuckle and that pisses my father off more because he shoots me a look.

"You can stay, but this," my father waves between the two of us, "is over."

I go to speak; however, my father turns quickly and walks away, not allowing me the chance. Why is he such an asshole?

Sighing, I turn my attention to East, who is staring at my father's retreating form. If looks could kill, my daddy would be on the ground in three seconds flat. There's no denying the hate in those eyes that are as dark as the night sky. Another sign that I should fear the man standing next to me.

Deciding to make the most of our time here, I reach for his hand. Those pitch-black eyes meet mine, then glance down at where we are connected.

"Let's get a drink."

"Water." He nods.

He never lets go of my hand as we make our way through the crowd. I kind of like it. His firm grip gives me to confidence to hold my head high as people stop and stare. I don't have the urge to run and hide. Instead, I smile slyly at a few guests.

When we finally reach the bar, I'm the first to order. "I'll take a martini, please."

"She'll have water. Make that two." East slides a twenty across the counter toward the bartender. I gape at him. Did he seriously just change my drink order?

"Stop staring at me. You'll thank me later."

"The hell I will." I don't know who he thinks he is. Acting like my father is something I will not be tolerating from him.

"Sir, please bring me a martini— "

I'm silenced when strong arms pull me in close. Lips brush my ear, sending chills down my spine. "I want you fully sober for later." He pulls back and winks before handing me a bottle of water.

Asshole.

I want to hate him.

I want to fuck him.

I want to forget him.

I want to remember him.

My mind is swimming with all thoughts that are East Sinclair that I don't hear him speak to me at first.

"Charla, did you hear me?"

"I'm sorry, I didn't."

"Now is not the time to think dirty thoughts. I have to go give my speech." The man in front of me smirks, chewing on his lip ring. Every bit of a bad boy.

He pulls me in once more, causing my heart rate to spike. And God, the smell of him.

"Let's get this over with, we have plans and I don't like to be kept waiting."

I swallow unable to form any coherent words. My entire body is on fire. How can one sentence have this effect on me?

After finding the circular table that was reserved for me, I take in the details. White silk covers the table and a vase full of yellow roses sits in the center surrounded by tiny tea light candles. I try to turn my attention to the podium; however, I'm distracted by Spencer, who sits down next to me.

He squeezes my leg. "Welcome to the lion's den. This should go well."

"I just need them to see, loud and clear."

"Oh, they see all right and they are both pissed." Spencer nods his head at the two men that have approached our table. Corey, being the asshole he is, sits down on my other side. It makes me internally cringe. My father sits directly across from me.

Corey leans over and places a kiss on my cheek, immediately causing me to pull back. I gawk at him. The nerve.

"Charla, don't you dare make a scene."

"Then tell Corey to keep to himself."

"What can't I kiss my beautiful bride to be?"

I laugh.

Spencer spits his drink back into the clear tumbler.

"Spencer, Charla, what has gotten into you two?"

With a fake smile plastered on my face, I shake my head. "Daddy, you and Corey are delusional. I want nothing to do with Corey."

That causes Spencer to choke again, and I give myself a silent pat on the back.

"Stop being a bitch, Charla," Corey snaps and squeezes my thigh hard. I try to yank my leg away, but he has too strong of a grip. It'll probably bruise due to me fighting him.

"Do you see this, father? This is the kind of man you want me with? One that forces himself on me and speaks to me in such a manner? Surely not."

"Corey, now is not the time. We don't need a show. Charla and that punk are giving the journalists enough to talk about."

"We have an agreement, remember?"

An agreement? What in the hell?

"Not now, Corey." My father nods to the podium. Following my father's line of sight, East is standing there, staring straight at us and if I didn't know any better, I'd say he's pissed. The tic in his muscular jaw tells me so.

Spencer stands suddenly and comes between us quickly. "Enough of this, take your hand off her. Now."

"Spencer," my father all but whispers. People glance our way. East is talking, but I have no idea what he's saying. Embarrassment floods me. All the eyes, Corey, Spencer, my father. It's too much. Once upon a time, I lived for attention. Those days are gone and right now I pray for the floor to open up so that it can swallow, and remove me from this nightmare that has become my life.

Spencer retreats because that's what he does when my father speaks his name in such a manner. I feel bad. I hate that my father has so much control. Too much. It needs to end, but how?

Corey continues to keep a grip on my thigh. Yup, definitely leaving a mark, there's no doubt now. Trying to forget that his grubby hands are marking my body, I brave a glance around the room. Luckily, most have turned their attention back to the strikingly hot man at the front of the room. I decide to try to give him my full attention. I need the distraction and East Sinclair is the perfect distraction. Especially as he begins to roll up his sleeves, exposing the ink that crawls up his arms and underneath the black material.

I hear a few gasps, whispers. They are shocked to see a wealthy businessman covered in tattoos. The largest donor of the night at that. I keep my eyes on East. He smirks. He did that on purpose. To rile up my father, to stick it to him.

I don't even pay attention to what East is saying up there. I can't focus. Not with his hard eyes on me. Let me rephrase, his eyes are trained on my thigh where Corey's hand still holds me.

"Mr. Richards, I'd take your hand off of Ms. Krauss."

Oh my god.

He didn't.

He did.

Everyone turns to look at us. Any second now the floor can open. Seriously.

My father clears his throat, a warning and like the good dog he is, Corey finally removes his hand and I immediately scoot my chair closer to Spencer.

"Thank you. Now where was I?" East clears his throat before continuing. "When I was informed of tonight's charity, I couldn't help but contribute. It hits close to home."

Interesting. Maybe he'll give me a little insight into what he meant as we were getting out of the limo.

"I came from an underprivileged home until my grandfather saved me." My hand covers my mouth in shock. I have so many questions. I want to know more about the mysterious man that captures my attention and my body like no one else.

That is until he starts to speak again after taking a sip of water.

"Thank you to my beautiful girlfriend, Charla..." East's words trail off as embarrassment hits my face. What the fuck? I can't believe he just called me out.

18

"It's been a pleasure to be a part of such an event." I nod and make my way back off the stage.

I hope fuck boy liked my little jab. I'm sure it'll have everyone in the room talking now, which was the point. To make it clear that she doesn't belong to that asshole who wouldn't take his hand off her. I watched from the stage as words were obviously exchanged between everyone seated. I'm not certain, but I think Spencer may have tried to defend her. It didn't work. Corey doesn't get the hint and neither does her control freak of a father. Hopefully now, though, they do.

As I approach the table, I notice several things at once. Corey and Mr. Krauss having what looks to be a heated conversation. Spencer looks like he wants to say something but is torn. Figures. No one speaks up because it just goes unheard.

And then there is Charla, who has stood abruptly and is now pushing past me, pissed off as can be.

What the hell?

I look at Spencer for an explanation, he just shrugs and spins the liquid in his tumbler around.

Turning to go after Charla, her father calls out, "Sinclair, a word."

I don't bother to look back or respond. I'm here for one thing and one thing only and now that I've done my part, I want my payment.

I catch up to Charla, who has just reached the entrance. Grabbing a hold of her small wrist, I stop her from going any further.

Instantly she turns and yanks her wrist free. "Don't touch me!"

Woah.

"What the hell did I do?"

"You." She stabs a finger at my chest. "Called me out in front of all those people."

Is she serious?

"You asked me to play the part of your boyfriend, did you not?"

"That didn't mean announce it to the world!"

"Look, you wanted your father and dickface to leave you alone. A public announcement was necessary. They weren't getting the hint."

She groans as she shakes her head at me. "Yeah, thanks for that."

I study the blonde bombshell that stands before me.

She's fucking gorgeous.

She's trouble.

Trouble I don't need.

As soon as I get my end of the deal, I'm out. The plan is to fuck her straight out of my system. I don't need all this bullshit. I do not have the time for it.

"Let's go." I make to grab her arm again, but she pulls back.

"Fuck you. I've called a cab."

"The hell you are taking a cab home. I'll be bringing you home."

"No, thanks. I think you've done enough for the evening."

She's making me angry. I don't like to play games. I step closer, surely, she hasn't forgotten. She will be coming home with me. And no, I'm not a creep like that dude back in the ballroom. I'm far from that. I just need to get Charla out of my system. She owes me this.

"In case you forgot." I pause as I watch the heat flare in her eyes. Good. I'm glad she is pissed at me. This will make for a good time. "You agreed to do whatever I want."

To my surprise, she laughs right in my face. Such a bitch, yet she makes my dick twitch. I can hardly wait to sink into her tight pussy.

She flicks her curls over her shoulder like the stuck-up princess she is before turning and walking right out the door. I let her. It makes the chase more exciting. It gets my blood pumping.

I follow her out, letting her think I have given up. She gets halfway down the walkway before I catch up and pin her against the closest car. I hope it's Corey's.

"Get off of me!"

"Is that what you really want, Charla?" I grind against her on purpose. I want her to feel how damn hard I am.

Her breath catches as she lets out a soft moan. Her hips push into mine. Just as I thought. And I won't lie and say I wouldn't take her right here. I would in a heartbeat just to teach her a fucking lesson, but I'm not that guy. Not tonight.

I nip at her neck, causing more whimpers from her beautiful mouth. God fucking her is going to be so good.

"I hate you, East." Her words are meant to pack a punch to my gut, but they are weak. Lust trails behind her words.

"I want you to hate me. You should hate me."

She pushes against my chest. I take a step back but not before dragging my teeth across her flesh.

Charla's breathing is heavy, her chest rising and falling quickly.

"How much do you want?"

"What?"

"I will pay you for this evening. I just want this night to be over."

Tilting my head to the side, I smirk. "It's not money that I'm wanting. Now let's go. No more wasting time."

Has she not realized that I make my own money? Did she already forget how much I just donated to her father's charity?

She must have because she turns to continue on her way.

I'm beginning to grow tired of the game of cat and mouse.

I snake my arm around her waist and push her up against the vehicle that is parked behind the one I just had her up against.

I kind of like that I'm leaving our mark.

With her front against the dark Bentley, I grind against her ass.

"Fuck you, East."

"Oh, I plan to fuck you. It's just going to be a matter of where."

I grab a bit of fabric that covers her hip and begin to pull it upward. Immediately, she grabs my hand, stilling me. Her gown is open in the back, dipping to just above her ass. No bra. I place my lips against her bare back but don't kiss her.

I don't kiss. Why do I have to remind myself of that when I'm with her?

"Not here. Please not here."

I smile against her skin. She just gave me the upper hand.

I let the thin fabric fall and slide my hand up her back and under her dress across her ribs. She shivers and goosebumps break out against her skin. I seriously enjoy the effect I have on Charla. She's like the perfect drug. A drug I can't seem to get enough of. After tonight, though, no more. I'm determined. I can't be getting addicted to her.

"East," Charla whispers as she rubs her ass against my dick and fuck me if it doesn't feel good.

I continue sliding my hand until I cup her breast. It's a tight fit. Her skintight dress leaves little room for movement, but I manage to take her pebbled nipple between my fingers and pinch her ever so slightly.

Her head falls back against my shoulder, allowing me access to her neck. Wasting no time, I sink my teeth in and then start sucking after each bite. I have no shame in marking her. Even though she is not mine. She'll never be mine, but I mark her anyway.

I keep up my assault until she reaches back and grabs me. Her grip is firm and suddenly the desire to have her hands wrapped around my cock is in the forefront of my mind.

I need to get her to the limo.

Now.

Ever so slowly, I remove my hand from her smooth skin and grab her hips pulling her against me. Breathing into her ear, "Time to go, Charla."

This time she doesn't resist. She allows me to walk her to my limo that's waiting.

As I help her in, I feel eyes on me, I turn back to see Corey standing on the steps. I wonder how long he has been there. How much did he see? Hopefully, he saw Charla melt like fucking putty at my touch.

Watching us like the stalker he is. The dude can't get any creepier. I smirk at him as I climb in. I hope he pictures me fucking Charla when he closes his eyes tonight.

19

EAST

The minute I climb in and shut the door, all thoughts of dickface are forgotten. Charla is sitting on the far side of the limo. Her dress does nothing to hide her hardened nipples. I bet if I stuck my hand up her dress she would be soaked.

But what's more, is how fucking hot she is. She's not just some dumb bombshell. No. She's fucking Charla Krauss.

I already know what I want as I shrug out of my blazer. I make quick work of removing my bowtie and undoing a few buttons on my dress shirt. Her eyes never leave my fingers, watching my every move. When I finally drop my hands to my belt, she bites her bottom lip while watching me undo it, pulling it through the loops, and dropping it on the seat next to me.

Very slowly, I undo the button on my slacks and pull the zipper down. I pause before springing my dick free. Instead, I leave Charla hanging, her eyes are filled with lust and that alone makes my dick twitch.

"Remove your thong."

Charla raises an eyebrow. Her mouth curls up into a smile that's far from innocent. "I'm not wearing one."

Ah, hell. My shocked expression leaves her laughing. This woman.

Making myself comfortable, I finally free my cock. I watch as Charla's tongue darts out, wetting her lips. Lips that are about to be wrapped about my dick.

"Suck my dick."

"Excuse me?"

"You heard me. Now suck my dick."

"You're a jerk," she states as she comes closer to me, dropping to her knees.

"We've established this. I warned you that I was not what you want."

She rolls her eyes at my words at the same time she takes my dick in her hand, stroking it slowly.

God, that alone feels good. Precum has already pooled at the head, and she wastes no time licking it up.

She continues teasing me. Stroking and licking me. I can't fucking take it. I want her mouth wrapped around me.

"That's not sucking my dick."

Charla sits back and glares at me. Fuck, I love pissing her off. I say nothing, instead, I put my hands behind my head and wait to see what she spits out.

"I deserve better. Far better."

"Again, I warned you." I nod to my erection. "It's not going to suck itself."

She comes back closer, digging her perfectly manicured nails into my thighs. So hard she'll probably draw blood. What she fails to realize is she can't hurt me. This kind of pain does nothing but make me crave more.

With her other hand gripping my dick firmly, her pink lips wrap around me. In an instant, I'm hooked on the drug that is Charla Krauss. Her lips are like morphine. I can't get enough; no dose will ever be enough.

And that's a problem.

Charla continues sucking in perfect rhythm. I don't want to stop her, but know if I don't, I'll be filling her mouth with my cum very soon.

20

East's tight grip on my hair causes my eyes to tear up and for some reason, I like it. Where he seems to induce pain, I seem to get turned on. Why am I like this? Is it normal?

Before I can overthink more, East yanks hard on my hair. His cock leaves my mouth with a popping sound. It's glistening, iron-hard, and even though I'm still so pissed at him, I wait in anticipation for what comes next.

"Sit on my dick, now, Charla."

"Fuck you."

"That's exactly what you are about to do."

Rolling my eyes, I hike my gown up to my hips exposing my bare skin. I watch as East's eyes darken as he takes me in. He likes what he sees. Which is a pity because after tonight, I plan to stay far away from him. He's proving to be too much trouble. He's not worth it.

I go to straddle him before lowering myself on him, but he puts a hand out stopping me in my tracks. With the same hand, his fingers lightly skim my stomach as they make their way lower. He dips one finger between my slick folds, causing me to whimper at his touch. I wish I didn't react to him the way I do, however, my body betrays me in that department. My body seems to want everything that East has to give.

He proceeds to rub circles on my clit, teasing me. It's torture. He brings me to the brink of an orgasm before stopping, removing his fingers. Through hooded eyes that never leave mine, he brings his finger to his mouth and very slowly sucks on it.

Fuck if it's not hot as sin to watch him.

"So sweet."

I'm dying for a release and here he is playing me. Killing me slowly.

After what feels like an eternity, he grabs my hips, pulling me to straddle him. I'm so wet, there's zero resistance when I sink down on his cock.

I throw my head back, he feels so good that all thoughts of anger dissipate as I ride him hard. His hands are still on my hips, digging in as he takes control of how fast I move.

I need to move faster, I need release.

"East," I moan bringing my hands to his hair, pulling it. Hard.

I see the fire in his eyes the minute I do. He's not the only one who can do rough. The sad thing is, he probably likes it. I pull a little harder.

"Fucking hell, woman." East removes my hands from his dark hair and pins them with one hand behind my back.

With his other hand, his thumb finds my swollen clit. He applies pressure before pinching it. I arch my back, hoping to reach that peak of pleasure.

East has other plans though. He removes his thumb and lifts me off of him in one swift move. The next thing I know, his cock is being shoved back in my mouth where he fucking cums without warning. Warm liquid hits the back of my throat and I swallow without thinking.

No man has ever done that to me. I've never had a guy finish in my mouth and that also means I've never swallowed before either. I was too good for that.

Until now.

East has some fucking nerve.

When my eyes look up at him, he wears the smile of a devil. No shame whatsoever. I watch astounded as he tucks his cock back into his slacks, and pulls up his zipper.

"We've arrived. Have a good night."

He's joking. I look fast out the window, sure enough, we are in front of my building.

That fucker.

This isn't over.

But it is because the driver has opened the door, holding his hand out for me.

"You're an asshole."

"I am."

I climb out and don't bother to look back. I'm too pissed, yet I refuse to let him see it. Each step is painful. My pussy is aching for a release that East denied me of.

No one and I mean no one has ever done that to me before. How dare he?

I really him.

————

After getting out of the limo, I immediately went to my room and grabbed my vibrator just so I could finish myself off. It did the job, but not in the way I really needed. I wanted to climb the highest mountain and then free fall straight into the dark waters that only East seems to create.

But no, that didn't happen. After I took the edge off, I ran a hot shower, like scorching hot. I felt the need to cleanse myself after everything.

Spencer has texted me several times, I've ignored each one. I'm not in the mood.

My father has also texted and called. I've ignored him too, so when the pounding comes at the front door, I assume it's him to lecture me on my unacceptable friend.

I take my sweet ass time. I really don't want to have this shit conversation. I'm fed up and over every single thing in my life.

When I pull the door open, I'm not expecting Spencer to be standing there.

He has a key, why not just come in?

"Um, hey, I didn't want to just intrude... in case..."

I turn and walk away. "He's not here."

"Oh." I hear the door shut and Spencer following behind. "So, how did the rest of the night go, you know after you stormed off?"

Sighing, I start making coffee. I need caffeine.

I say nothing as I stare at the coffee pot. What's there to say? That I sucked East's cock in the back of a limo, then rode him until he threw me off and stuck his cock back in my mouth to finish.

Yeah, no thanks.

"I take it, from your silence that you've heard the news then?"

The hair raises on my arms. News?

"What news?" I snap, not meaning to direct it at my best friend. He flinches and shakes his head looking at his phone.

"Charla, someone talked to the press. Someone shared photos."

"What?" I snatch the cell from him and regret it instantly. This can't be happening.

No.

No.

No.

I don't even read the words, no I'm stuck on the image. It's a photo of East all over me outside of his club. I'm up against the wall, his face is buried in my neck. I know exactly what he was doing in that moment.

He was marking me.

Marks that I covered the next day with makeup. I didn't want to look like *that girl*. Doesn't matter now because I am *that girl*.

They say a picture is worth a thousand words. I can't help but wonder if the lustful expression on my face can actually be described in that many words. Probably not, but everyone who looks at that photo will know exactly what I was feeling at that moment.

No doubt about it.

East pleasuring me. It was meant to be a private moment and now everyone and their mom will know.

I sink down on the bar stool and Spencer wraps me into a tight hug.

"Don't worry, this will blow over, Char."

But will it?

That would be a big fat because more pounding sounds at my door and there's only one person that could be.

My father.

21

CHARLA

"Spencer, I'm going to ask you to leave. I need to speak with my daughter."

How my father speaks to Spencer makes me flinch. He's angry and if I had to guess, he saw the reports too.

Spencer gives me a questioning look. He doesn't want to leave me alone with my father. Honestly, I don't want him to leave me either. But this is my problem and I'm not about to drag another person into this disaster. Having East involved is enough.

"I'll call you later." I plaster on my signature smile. Spencer's eyes narrow, he can read me like an open book. He nods once and walks out.

"Your behavior of recent is not acceptable, and I'm putting a stop to it right now."

So typical, he jumps right, no holding back.

Taking a sip of my coffee, I just look at him. I'm sure he'll continue on his rant any minute.

"Are you listening to me?"

"Daddy, I've listened to you my entire life. Have you ever listened to me?"

"Charla, don't give me that attitude. Have you even seen the reports? You and that scum are plastered everywhere for the world to see! It's shameful and makes you look like trash."

No shit, Father. I know it's plastered everywhere. The question is, who took the damn picture and shared it with the piranhas?

Walking over to my large windows, I stare out at the ocean. God, how I wish I could be swept out in the current right now.

"This stops now! I'll have my people do damage control."

"You mean you'll have them make up some bullshit lie." I turn to face my father. "Isn't that what they are good at? Twisting the truth how you see fit? Don't bother. The truth is out there and I'm sick of living a lie."

"Living a lie? I have given you a great life. I set you up to thrive and here you are throwing it away for some guy who runs a strip club."

"No, Daddy, you set me up for whatever it is you want. What about what I want? What about the life I want to live? Do you not realize, had you stopped pushing Corey at me, I would have never bothered with East? That's your fault. You wouldn't listen." Tossing my hands up in frustration, I turn and face the ocean again.

"Don't you try to turn this around on me. Corey is exactly what you need in your life. You need someone who is in control of their situation because you obviously aren't in control of yours. Just look at the photo!"

My father is pissed. His yelling tells me he's not going to

let this matter go. Not until I agree to whatever bullshit he wants.

"Whatever you say, Daddy. What is it that I need to do to get you off my back?"

"Charla! I will not have this. We are going to do an article that states that isn't you in the photo. It must be someone who looks similar. I'll have it submitted by noon. You will sign this." He slams paperwork on the counter. I didn't even see him come in with anything in his hand. Knowing Daddy though, he had it tucked away in his coat.

I walk over and start to read the black words printed perfectly on thick white paper.

Shall have no contact...
East Sinclair...

My eyes dart around until it registers that my father wants me to sign a no-contact order against East Sinclair.

I look up and glare at him. "You're joking, right? You can't be serious?"

"Sign it, now." My lovely father holds out a pen for me to take.

I take it and the paper and walk straight over to the trash where I toss it straight in.

"Charla Ann!" My father slams his hands down on the granite, causing me to jump. I don't let my fear get to me though. I need to stand my ground or at least try to.

"Father, I will not sign a no-contact order that you surely obtained illegally. I want no part in it."

"I do whatever it is I need to do to keep you from him."

Ha! "That's perfect. How about you do the same with Corey."

"Corey is a good man."

"No, Corey is a pig. I need to shower and get my day started. Have your people tell the newspapers whatever it is that will make your cold heart happy, but I will not be signing shit."

Holding my head high, I make my way to the entryway and hold the door open, letting my father know he's no longer welcome here.

"You are making a huge mistake. I hope you are prepared to make new living arrangements because I will not stand for this."

"I can afford to pay for this place myself, you just choose to pay for it."

"Your money is of no use. You see this suite is in my name and if you don't abide by my rules, you'll have to make new living arrangements. You have one week to sign the contract. After that, I'm having the locks changed."

My asshole of a father walks away, leaving me standing there in shock, mouth opened wide.

I slowly shut my door, locking it. I need to catch my breath. I need to think. Surely this condo isn't only in his name. I signed the forms.

After taking a few minutes to gather my thoughts and try to calm down, I go into my office and open the drawer on my desk. In it is multiple files of important documents.

After shuffling through to find the lease agreement, I look over the documents. Some of it doesn't make sense at first. However, as I reread the words, I see that the lease is in fact in my father's name only with a stipulation agreement attached. That stipulation states that I, Charla Krauss, may be required to vacate the premises at any time with no notice.

Why would my father create such an agreement?

Or better yet, how did I just sign on the dotted line without reading?

Because, silly me, I listen to Daddy when he says sign here instead of reviewing a single thing he has ever handed me.

I've got to go down to management and see what can be done about this. Hopefully, it can't stick even though it is my signature. There's got to be something they can do.

Wishful thinking. Knowing my father, he's got his claws in deep and that means I'll be royally fucked if he actually decides to evict me.

This new reality is showing me another side of my father and what kind of man he truly is.

I'm not sure I like who he is anymore.

22

I think I've finally fucked Charla out of my system. After the other night and the look on her face as I so coldly dismissed her, I'm sure she has finally seen what kind of man I am. It's best she stays away. It's best I stay away.

"Boss?" Rian slides a water my way.

"Yes?"

"Have you seen the news, social media?"

"No, I don't pay attention to that shit."

I watch as Rian swallows thickly before nodding his head. "You may want to." With that, he turns and goes back to getting things in order for tonight.

I don't bother to check what's happening in the gossip world. I don't care. My business is more important.

Flipping open the back door cameras, I see it's clear. I switch to the front thinking there will be nothing there as well since it is still quite early. Just when I'm about to exit without really looking, I catch the glimpse of blonde hair.

Fucking Charla.

I guess my shit stunt didn't scare her enough. I'll have

Marc tell her to leave because if I go out there, I'm afraid I'll want to stick my dick back in her mouth.

Her perfect lips. My dick twitches at the thought.

Maybe I'll tell her myself after all.

My camera is still on when I go to stand, movement on the screen catches my eye. What I'm not expecting to see is a guy next to her. He's standing close. A little too close.

Why does that bother me?

Before I know what I'm doing, I'm up off the stool, storming toward the red doors. I pull the handle harder than necessary and step out.

What in the fuck is this shit?

To my surprise, it's not Charla, but Scarlett. The two women have a striking resemblance. It almost throws me off until the asshole next to her speaks.

"Well, look who it is?"

I want to swipe the sadistic smile right off of Corey's face. I won't, though, I'm a fucking professional and I won't have him ruining the empire I've built.

"You are not welcome here, you need to leave."

I turn to Scarlett, who looks nervous. "Lettie, inside."

She hurries away toward the door just as Corey calls out. "It was nice talking with you, *Scarlett*." Scarlett freezes at his words. She looks back, not at him. No, her eyes go straight to mine. She knows I know. The bastard used her real name. There's a rule here at The Red Society, we don't do first names. Ever. No matter the circumstance. It's to keep the women safe. She broke that rule.

"Inside, now." I point to the door before directing my attention back to Corey.

"You are not welcome at this establishment. Do not let me find you here again. Understand?"

"Loud and clear." He smirks and climbs into his car.

Something isn't right. I feel it deep down. Which is odd because I haven't felt this way in many years. Not since my grandfather rescued me. Not since the day I moved into his home.

After storming back inside, I go to the bar to retrieve my water before calling Scarlett to my office. We need to talk.

"Did you look at the headlines yet?" Rian calls out as I get to the black staircase that heads upstairs.

I had forgotten all about the gossip shit the minute I walked outside. I continue upstairs but open my phone along the way.

MAYOR'S DAUGHTER DATING STRIP CLUB OWNER.

There's a photo under the headline. It's of Charla and me, outside of my club. The night I had her up against the wall. My face is buried in her fucking neck. Not going to lie, this photo is fucking hot.

My erection straining against my zipper won't let me deny it either. The problem is, who fucking took this picture? Who the fuck was out there? No vehicles pulled in. It had to be someone that was already here.

Scarlett.

Red. I see fucking red. After everything I've done for the girl, this is her way of giving thanks. My fist nails the intercom.

"Scarlett, my office. Now." I don't even bother to hide the anger that is radiating from me.

I'm too mad to sit. I pace behind my desk instead. I've done so much for Scarlett. She was dealt one horrible mother and I've gone over and beyond to make sure she had food in her mouth and a roof over her head. Granted it's a shit hole, but that's because she still feels the need to give her mom money for her shit habits.

"Sir, you wanted to see me?" The fear in Scarlett's eyes is clear as day. Good. She should be scared. Her job is on the line.

"Sit."

She does as she is told. She twists her hands together as she places them in her lap. I'm so angry I'm not even sure where to start.

"Why were you outside with Corey Richards?"

She opens her mouth to speak but then closes it.

"Now, Scarlett. I don't have time for this."

"He, um... offered me a position."

The fuck he did not!

Pausing at my chair, I rest both hands on it, outstretching my arms. "He offered you a job?" I need clarification.

"Yes, sir."

"Why on earth would you give him your real name? You don't know him from shit."

"I... I didn't. He already knew it. He called me by it as I was walking in."

The pacing starts again while I process her words. Why the fuck would he want a stripper to work for him? Unless maybe to get back at Charla, but I can't see Mr. Krauss being accepting of that. Not one bit. And how the fuck does he know her real name? Shit isn't adding up. And what about the photo of me and Charla?

"Why did you take that photo of Charla and me outside and submit it to the tabloids?"

Confusion crosses her face. "I'm sorry, what photo?"

"Don't play with me. Why did you submit it to the damn tabloids?" I can't help but slam my hands down on my desk. I'm so fucking frustrated.

"I don't know what you are talking about. I don't know anything about a photo."

Tilting my head, I study the blonde dancer seated in front of me. She truly looks confused. What's more though, is how much she looks like Charla. Same hair, except Scarlett's isn't as bright. They have similar facial features, same color eyes.

It's bizarre and I can't stop staring at her. How have I never noticed this?

"Sir, what are you talking about?"

I need to focus. "Give me your phone."

"It's in the dressing room."

I nod, of course it is. Picking up my phone, I page out for Marc.

"What's up, boss?"

"Please bring me Scarlett's cell. It's in her dressing room."

"Ten-four."

My eyes go back to the blonde whose leg is now bouncing with nervous energy. I can't tell if that makes her guilty.

"Scarlett, is there anything you are keeping from me?"

"No, no, sir. I swear I don't know anything about a photo."

Two minutes later, Marc walks in with Scarlett's phone. She unlocks it without hesitation too.

There's nothing. No photos. Not one single photo. I even check her trash folder and archive. I even go as far as looking through her emails. The problem is, she has no email account set up on this phone, which I might add, is a dinosaur. Not surprising, though, given her life.

"You have no photos at all?"

She shrugs her shoulders like it's no big deal. "What would I take photos of?"

She has a point. A valid fucking point and that's pathetic. She really should want more for her life. Perhaps that is what Corey is trying to offer her. I doubt it though.

"Am I being fired?" Scarlett's voice breaks, snapping me out of my raging thoughts. I look at her, she's trembling, but damn does she look like the blonde I can't get out of my head.

"If I catch you associating with that piece of shit again you will be. Don't you ever bring him here again."

"But I, I didn't bring him here. He was already here when I arrived."

"Is that so?"

What the fuck is that mother fucker up to? Scarlett nods, probably too afraid to speak. She even nods like Charla.

How is that even possible?

"Tell me something about yourself, Scarlett."

"I'm sorry?"

"Tell me something personal? Something only you know."

"Um, there's not much to tell. You already know my mom worked here years ago."

"She did. She ever mention your dad or past relationships?" I know I'm going out on a limb here, however, I want to know.

"Sometimes when she is drinking, she'll mention stuff. Most of it makes no sense."

"Like?"

"I don't know. Once she mentioned my birth dad being wealthy. Another time she mentioned he was famous, or like a judge, something like that, and that he had my sibling. I usually don't pay attention when she rambles. It's probably all lies anyway." She tosses her hand out and laughs at that last bit. Exactly like someone else.

I'm not laughing. Not one fucking bit.

23

CHARLA

I haven't signed the contract. I refuse to sign it. I refuse to sign a lie that makes East out to be a monster. I mean, he is a monster when he takes my body and owns it like no other. Regardless of what he does to my body, he's far from the monster my father wants to paint him out to be. I may be a rich girl, but I still have morals and I will not ruin East like that.

I've avoided my father for the past few days. He has texted daily, only asking if the papers were ready to be picked up. No how are you or anything like that. He only cares about one thing so I don't bother to respond.

Instead of worrying about what my father may or may not do, I've thrown myself into work. I arrive early and leave late.

Like right now.

It's well after five and here I am plugging away. It's better than going home and pacing until the wine kicks in.

"Charla?" Spencer's voice calls from down the hall.

"Yeah, Spence."

He lets out a sigh. "Promise me you will close up and go home within the next thirty minutes?"

"Uh, yeah, sure." The lie rolls off of my tongue easily. I have been staying until at least eight and tonight will be no different.

I hear him grumbling as his voice fades off into the distance. He hates that I've been staying late. Really, he should be impressed with all the accounts I've tackled and have handed over to him.

Taking a deep breath, I take a minute to stretch my arms. When I told Spencer what transpired between my father and me, he immediately told me to pack my bags and come stay with him until my father cools down. I just can't bring myself to do that though. I'm an adult and need to handle my own problems.

The issue is, I don't know how to fix this. And I still don't know who took that photo to begin with. It is very concerning because if one photo was taken, chances are there are more. It's only a matter of time before more will surface. What if someone snapped photos of East fucking me at my car? Of me screaming out his name as he pulled my hair while slamming into me?

I grow embarrassed just thinking about it.

Then there's this nagging feeling in the back of my mind. What if East sent those photos in himself to be an asshole? To scare me off? They were taken outside of his club after all. I know the photo didn't come from his security cameras. The angle is from the parking lot. Someone was definitely out there and that weighs on my mind too.

I want to ask East about the photo, but like my father, I'm avoiding him too. I needed space to clear my head. Let's face it, when East is around me it's like he opens the window, and all intelligent thoughts fly out. My good girl image goes out the window and a side of me I'm not sure of comes out to play.

I will admit, that I miss how alive I feel when he is around. I miss the things he does to my body.

But dammit, I could have gone without the shit storm it has created.

I finally head out after eight. Spencer will probably be annoyed. Oh well.

As I head into the parking garage, there are very few cars out here. I don't even pay much attention until I hear a quiet whimper. Was that a woman? Suddenly feeling on edge, I glance around but see no one. I pick up the pace, keys already in hand.

After getting in my SUV, I lock the doors right away. I check all mirrors before backing out of my spot. Maybe I was hearing things.

As I start to drive toward the exit, a person steps out from behind a vehicle. A female. She looks like a deer in headlights staring at me. She looks frightened.

I pull up closer to her and crack my window." Are you okay?"

The woman, whose hair is blonde, just nods and glances behind her. She stands there nervously, wearing a white mini dress that is tight as can be. Her tits and curves on display for the world.

"Do you need a ride somewhere?" I don't know why I ask, there's just something about her. She looks almost scared.

"She doesn't need a ride." A male's voice comes from behind her. I know that voice. Before it registers, Corey steps up behind her, placing his hand on her hip. The pretty woman freezes in place. She is clearly uncomfortable in his presence. So typical of him though. He's a pig after all.

Choosing to ignore him I ask one more time, "You sure you're okay?"

She nods again, not speaking.

Okay then. I study the two of them. It gives me this uneasy feeling. She looks familiar, like me in a sense. Is that how I looked on Corey's arm? Her body language seems all wrong. Maybe she's having second thoughts about going with him.

Been there. Done that.

I shake my head and go about my way, but not without checking them in my rearview mirror several times before turning out of the garage.

The entire way home, I picture her face. Her features and how nervous she looked. She truly looked familiar. I tell myself that it's because Corey is obsessed with me that he had to go find a woman who looked like me. Maybe she was the chick on his arm at the restaurant or maybe she has attended one of Daddy's events. It doesn't matter anyway. I just truly hope she will be okay.

I awake to Spencer shaking me, almost violently. "Char! Wake up! You have to see this shit!"

I shrug him off me and rollover. "Not now, I need sleep." I'm beyond tired. Sleep didn't come easily last night. I kept thinking of that woman with Corey. I mean it completely consumed my thoughts to the point I almost called Corey more than once just to make sure he didn't do something he shouldn't have.

"This is serious! The pap is eating this shit up!" He sounds excited. Too excited and it's way too early for that shit.

"Spencer, go away." I try to burry my head under my pillow but he's quick and snatches it away.

"Hey!" I shout and go to swat him but stop dead in my tracks and he holds his phone out in my face.

STRIPPER CLAIMS TO BE WOMAN WITH STRIP CLUB OWNER

What? I sit straight up. My eyes fly to Spencer's green gaze. He looks angry, annoyed… I'm not sure. He nods back to his phone and my eyes follow just as his thumb swipes across the screen revealing yet another article.

NOT THE MAYOR'S DAUGHTER? WHOS IS THIS STRIPPER?

Confusion clouds my thoughts. "What is this?"

"A dancer from The Red Society is claiming to be you in the leaked photo." He nearly grinds his teeth together. Anger is evident in his tone.

I shake my head. That doesn't make any sense. Why would that make my best friend angry? Why would a dancer claim that she is me?

"Listen, coffee first, then explain." Falling back onto my bed, I rub my eyes. Shit, it's too early for this crap.

"Already done. Coffee is in the kitchen. Now get up."

I groan while climbing out of bed.

I need to see what shit storm awaits now.

24

CHARLA

After consuming way too much coffee, I'm finally awake. Like I'm jittery from all the caffeine. Nothing that I have read makes sense. Why is some stripper at the club claiming to be me? It's not adding up. Did East put her up to it? So many questions and no answers.

Spencer has been pacing my kitchen. More times than I can count. Something is up with him.

"Yo, Spence... want to talk about it?" He stops, studies and stares at me to the point that it almost makes me uncomfortable.

"Spence?"

He shakes his head. "Yeah, sorry, just trying to piece all this together."

"Why?"

"Because you're my friend."

"Yeah, but you're acting like this is a huge deal to you." I mean I get that it's a big deal. Red flags are raised. There's something more though. At least for him.

"I'm worried your dad or Corey played a role."

I nod. Spencer has a point. It wouldn't surprise me if they had something to do with this article. I didn't sign the papers, and this could be Daddy's way of fixing shit. His way.

"I'm going to text East."

I've been so good at not reaching out. I've stayed strong. Maybe he knows something I don't.

Hey… did you see the article?

I watch as the dots that indicate he's typing, pop up almost immediately. It makes me both excited and anxious.

Of course, I saw it, Charla.

This won't look good for his business. I quickly type out another text.

And?

After hitting send, I glance back at Spencer. He's no longer pacing. Nope. His hands are braced on the counter and he's staring again. His green eyes, which are lighter than East's, nearly penetrate my skin and not in the good kind of way.

"Spencer, you are starting to scare me."

He pushes off the counter and rounds it to come in front of me. On instinct, I take a step back.

"Spence." The whisper barely leaves my lips because in the next moment, Spencer steps into my personal space. All thoughts of waiting for a response from East are quickly forgotten. Spencer is so close I can feel his breath on me. He doesn't touch me though. He just keeps staring at my face. His head tilts to the side and he squints his eyes slightly.

I can't take it, the silence, his closeness. I take another step back.

"Don't, I'm sorry, Char... it's just your eyes..." He trails off, not finishing his thoughts.

His words come out of left field. Raising my eyebrow, I go to question, but he places a finger over my lips.

"Just give me a minute."

If my heart wasn't racing before, it certainly is now.

The front door opens quickly, followed by a slam. We both turn to see East Sinclair standing there. The first thing I notice is how fucking good he looks. His hair is a mess, black shirt has the first three buttons undone, allowing me a glimpse of the artwork that is across his chest. His black jeans hug his hips perfectly.

The second thing I notice is his facial expression. His eyes trained on Spencer. He's angry. Like really angry.

"East? What are you doing here?" I don't know why I ask, I'm pretty sure he is here to discuss said article.

"Step away from her now." His words shoot venom straight at Spencer. Spencer doesn't flinch at all. He doesn't listen to East.

After what feels like forever, my friend finally takes a step back. He shakes his head, turns, and walks toward East.

East shocks me by grabbing Spencer's arm. "Did you have something to do with this?"

"No, I did not. How dare you assume such a thing? If it wasn't for you, she wouldn't be in this fucking mess."

A million thoughts, questions swirl through my mind. Why would Spencer have a role in this?

Spencer shrugs out of East's grip and walks out. He leaves me standing there completely confused.

Meanwhile East wastes no time. He locks the door and heads straight for me. I don't move, I'm frozen in place.

"Did he hurt you?"

What? Is he serious?

He is.

I can practically feel the anger rolling off him in waves.

"Answer me, now!" He snaps. It causes me to jump.

"No... no, he didn't."

"What the fuck was he doing?"

"Um, I don't know."

"That's not good enough, Charla. What was he doing? Why was he so close to you?" He jerks my chin up to look at him.

"I... told you... I don't know. He just kept staring at me."

My words must satisfy him. He loosens his grip on me but never takes his eyes off of me though. It's like he's studying me too. Just like Spencer.

I take a deep breath. East smells good. A subtle woodsy scent.

Shaking my head, I step out of East's grip. I've had enough of the crazy. I walk over to the windows that look out into the ocean. I could use some clarity in my life. Ever since East came into the picture, I haven't had an ounce.

"I need answers. I want answers."

"I don't have any." East's words hit the back of my neck

as he pulls my hair to the side. I stand completely still as his fingers graze over my skin.

It gives me flashbacks of when he took me against the French doors.

His hand grips the back of my neck, pressing my face against the cool glass. I should be alarmed. I keep waiting for the fear to come. To be afraid of his actions. It hasn't come. Something must be wrong with me. Everything with East is intense and that for some reason excites me. Makes me feel alive.

"You've caused me a hell of a lot of problems. You know that?"

I know I've caused a lot of issues. Well, my father and Corey have. But it falls on me, so I say nothing. What is there to say?

Just as his lips touch my skin, surely to mark me, the sound of a lock turning barely registers before the door opens.

25

EAST

The sound of the door snaps me out of what I was about to do to Charla.

"What the hell is this?"

I don't even bother to turn toward the voice. I already know who it is. The one and only Stefan Krauss. His voice is like nails on a damn chalkboard. I can't fucking stand his voice. Or him if I'm being truthful.

He's a piece of shit in my book. Especially for what he is doing to Charla.

"Daddy, it's not what you— " Charla quickly steps away from me.

"Save it, Charla. It looks like you are still disobeying me and I take it you still haven't signed the document."

I watch Charla, gaging her reaction. She surprises me when she stands a little straighter, holds her head higher.

"You saw me throw the paperwork away. I refuse to sign a lie. I will not have any part of it."

God, what is her father up to now? I am certain he had to have a part in the article. Him and the fucker that follows him around like a lost dog.

"You continue to disappoint me. I assume, then, you are ready to vacate this suite."

What in the ever-loving fuck?

"Are you really going to throw me out? Knowing full well I can afford to pay for this? I don't need your money."

"Think of it as teaching you a lesson. I'll give you three days." The fucker turns to leave, but Charla runs up and stops him.

"Three days! How am I supposed to find a new place and pack in such a short amount of time? Are you crazy?"

I'm glad to see she is learning to stand up for herself. I didn't think she had it in her but seeing her stand up to that prick, well, it turns me on to the point I have to discreetly adjust myself.

"You've left me no other choice. You have created a huge mess, and I will not stand for it."

I knew Charla's father was an asshole. This brings out an entirely new side. Just as cruel.

"You'll stay with me." I blurt the words out without really thinking through that process of what it means for her to be in my personal space. Women aren't allowed in my personal space. Yet, I feel like stabbing the knife deeper into Stefan's salty wound and the look on his face tells me I stabbed him deeply.

Red creeps from his neck up to his jaw, cheeks. I hit a fucking nerve.

Good.

"You were told to stay away from my daughter. You are scum."

"Scum that is taking your daughter in because you are throwing her out like yesterday's trash."

Little does he know, I can play his bullshit game. If he thinks he can call the shots, he has another thing coming.

He has no idea the wrath that I can and will bring to the table.

I hold his evil stare while noticing the veins bulging in his neck. It's evident he has quite the temper and doesn't like when shit is thrown back in his ugly ass face. How is Charla so gorgeous? The opposite of him?

Speaking of Charla. Her emerald eyes are wide as they stare at me. I nod my head for her to come to me. She does so without question. She doesn't hesitate or even look back at her father. No, instead she walks straight up to me and fucking lays her lips on mine.

She kisses me hard, forcing me to open my mouth. I don't kiss. For some stupid reason, I give in when it comes to this woman. And since I want to stick it to dear dad once more, I wrap my arms around her and grab a handful of her ass. That'll show him.

"Motherfucker," I hear her father say along with some other bullshit ramblings. I pay no attention. Not until Charla's lips leave mine abruptly.

"What are you doing?!" she practically screams in her father's face.

He pulled her away from me.

That's not going to fly with me.

Not today.

Catching her wrist, I pull her behind me, moving to stand toe to toe with the bully.

I have about two inches on her father. He's shorter, rounder. His pupils dilate. He realizes I'm no match for him. See where he let himself go, I have not. I stay in shape and eat healthier. That much is obvious. Just because I have the cash to throw around doesn't mean it's okay to let myself go like the motherfucker standing in front of me.

He knows it too.

"I'm calling security. This man is not allowed on my property."

Ha. I laugh in his face. Figures he would stoop to a new low.

"You're being ridiculous, Daddy. I can't believe you are being like this."

I watch with humor as he takes his phone out and calls security. I'll gladly wait until they arrive.

"East." Charla steps around to face me. She looks exhausted. "You should go before security arrives. I'll be fine." Her tiny fingers wrap around my bicep, giving it a squeeze.

"I demand you to stop touching him, Charla."

"And I demand you to stop acting like I'm a child. You can't control me."

Charla's father chuckles. It's sadistic. I don't like it one bit. I almost open my mouth to interrupt, her, but the damn door opens yet again.

Security has arrived.

The guy has to be around my age. Unlike Charla's father, he is in shape, though I have no desire to hurt him.

"Mr. Krauss, Charla, is this the man you wish to have removed?"

"Yes!"

"No!"

Both speak in unison, and I can only laugh which causes all three to look at me.

Confusion.

Rage.

Shock.

"Ross, this is a friend of mine. Please don't pay my father any mind."

"Like hell, Charla. This is my condo. My name is on the

deed, look it up if you must. Then remove him." Stefan sticks his nose up as if the mention of me makes him physically sick. I hope I do. Because truth be told, that excuse of a father makes me sick. He reminds me of my mother. My blood boils. I haven't felt anger over my mother in some time now. Charla's father triggered something. I don't like it. I need space. I need it now.

"There will be a car waiting out front for you, Charla when you're ready."

Without another glance, I shove past her prick father and walk out.

I phone Burns and let him know to wait for Charla. I hang up without saying anything else.

I just offered Charla a place to stay. That wasn't my brightest move. It seems when she is around my judgment becomes clouded.

I promised myself after I was free of my mother, I would never allow another person to have any control over me so what the fuck did I just get myself into?

———

I left Charla's drama behind and went straight to the one place that brings me comfort.

The Red Society.

Ironic, I know, but I take pride in what I have built here. I took a sinking ship and repaired it.

I go straight to my office and page for Scarlet. I want answers and I want them right now.

A timid knock comes minutes later. "Sir?"

"Come in." I grind my teeth together to keep from screaming at her to just fucking come in. I called her to come here, I already know it is her. Jesus fuck.

One glance at her tells me she knows about the news article. That she probably had a hand in it. She's visibly shaking, her lips are already trembling.

Scratch that.

I know she did, and I know those fuckers played a part too. I'm so close to blowing up.

"Why, Scarlett? After all I have ever done for you. Why are you trying to destroy me? Did that bastard put you up to it?" I stand behind my desk, to irate to fucking sit.

"Sir, I'm sorry. I know you have done so much for me. Still do. Am I..." She hiccups as the first tears stream down her face. "Am I being fired?"

"You didn't answer my questions. Why did you do it?"

"I didn't want to. I didn't really. Honest. That man offered me a lot of money to say it was me in the photo. I figured it would be no big deal."

"How much did he offer you?"

"Ten thousand. Mr. Sinclair, you know I need that money. You know how beneficial it would be."

Figures that bastard would offer her some crazy amount. Scarlett is desperate. Tired and desperate. It's like dangling a fresh piece of meat in front of a lion and expecting it to just lay there and look at it, never striking.

"Did he come through with the money?"

Scarlett's head drops as she shakes it. What a prick. So, he promised her money and never paid up. Now she's at risk of losing everything. How stupid could she be?

"He never paid you? For lying?" I finally lose it and slam my hands on my desk, causing her to jump.

"He, he promised he would send payment as soon as the article was printed. I am... um... waiting."

"Fucking hell!" I pull at my hair. This is insane. I don't have time for such shit.

"Go home, Scarlett."

"What? am... I... No, please no. Don't fire me."

"I didn't say I was firing you. I told you to go home. Go home before I fire you. You deserve to be fired. Fucking fired to never return."

Scarlett is full-on crying now. I don't care. Not one fucking bit. She betrayed me. This club. When she makes no move to leave, she kills the last bit of my patience.

"Leave now!"

With that, she stands fast, nearly knocking over the chair. She rushes to the door and pauses.

"I'm so sorry, sir."

"If he contacts you, and I mean contacts you at all. You call me right away. Understood?"

"Yes, sir."

The minute the door shuts, I sink into my chair. I never have drama at this establishment. None. There's a reason for it. Those fucking reporters will probably be camped out across the street for the next two weeks. Trying to grasp at any gossip they can. Fucking snakes.

I page Marc.

An emergency meeting will be held directly after the doors are locked. No one will be speaking to the fucking press. Not on my watch.

26

CHARLA

East's driver has been driving us for about thirty minutes now. It has me wondering just where East Sinclair lives and why so far away.

The driver makes a right turn and I catch the tail end of a private drive sign. The driveway is paved and seems to go on for a while. Large oaks dripping with Spanish moss line each side as we continue. Not a palm tree in sight. Such a vast difference from my side of town.

After what seemed like twenty minutes, hell maybe it really was that long, a house comes into view. Well, let me rephrase the word house. It's more than a house. A two-story mansion is more fitting, complete with a courtyard driveway.

Fuck.

Not even my father's house is this elegant. Nor is Corey's. Just the thought of them sends shivers down my spine and not in a good way.

The driver, Burns I think, opens the door and holds out a hand for me to take. He is a patient man. I take my time getting out. I'm filled with complete shock.

East Sinclair lives here.

The bad boy who is hot and cold lives here and he's agreed to let me stay here.

With him.

"Ma'am, follow me and I'll give you the tour."

Nodding, I follow the older gentleman while trying to take everything in. The front of the home is a blend of red brick and cream stucco. Massive windows and two large front doors, black with stained glass windows. If I had to guess, I'd say the doors were made of wrought iron.

Burns opens the door and steps aside to let me in and let me just say that I never pictured East's home to look so... perfect.

Holy shit.

It's simple and yet that is what makes it perfect.

From the entryway straight ahead is the massive staircase, black marble. I run my fingers along the black banister as I follow the driver up the stairs. The all-black vibe completes the dark man I have come to know. I shouldn't be surprised that his taste is dark. He owns a strip club, after all.

When we arrive at the top of the stairs, Burns heads to the right. I pause, wondering what's to the left. A long, dark hallway. There are windows on the right, but they are covered with dark curtains, allowing no sun to shine through. All the doors on the opposite side are shut. How odd.

"Miss?"

Crap, I'm supposed to be following him. My face heats. "I'm sorry, coming."

I pick up my pace and catch up to the older man. He wears a blank expression, but his eyes twinkle. He clears his throat before speaking.

"That's Mr. Sinclair's side. Stay on this side. He does not let anyone other than the cleaner go over to that side." He continues on his way down the hall until we reach the very last door. Really? East is putting me in the last room. Furthest away from him. Not that it should even matter. Or maybe the rest of the rooms are taken. Do others live here? My mind runs wild with possible scenarios.

Burns opens the black door and gestures for me to go in. I do so, and he just waits at the door allowing me a minute.

This room is massive. Bigger than mine, that's for sure. A bed sits in the middle of the far end, between two windows. It too is covered in black. I'm beginning to think East doesn't do any other color.

"He wanted you to have the best view and a private bathroom. I hope this will suit you."

Wait... what?

I turn to face the man for a minute, but he gives nothing away. Turning my attention back to the room, that's when I notice that there are windows are three sides. The two that the bed sits between. There are two on the west side and two on the east. I walk to the west side and open the curtains. There's a balcony and this gives me a view of the front of the house. I can see the long driveway, but what I notice the most is, is the trees. All the greenery. A vast difference of my view back at my condo.

Pulling the curtains closed, I walk to the opposite side and open those curtains. This gives me a completely different view. One that consists of a courtyard and a very large lap pool.

It makes me sad to think I didn't bring my bikini.

I peek out of one of the windows by the bed. Nothing but oaks and moss. It's quite beautiful.

I turn back to Burns, is he smiling?

"I'll show you the rest of the house now. If you would like."

Again, I do nothing but nod. I'm still in a bit of shock.

We head back down to the first floor. There's a sitting area off to the corner near the front door. Burns leads me to what appears to be an open floor plan. Living room that flows right into the kitchen and dining space. Perfect for entertaining. Not that I think East does any type of entertaining. Then again, this man has shocked me with his house. He could have orgies here for all I know.

The walls are bare except for a few abstract paintings. It's the only pop of color I have noticed since stepping foot into the home of darkness himself. Even the kitchen consists of black cabinets. White granite counters and a white stone backsplash.

The living room, you guessed it, black leather couches and a white shag rug.

"Well, miss, what do you think?"

"He has a nice house."

He nods once, the twinkle still in his eyes. "If you'll excuse me, I'm going to retrieve your bags and bring them up to your room."

"Does East know any other color other than black and white?" I joke to Burns. I couldn't help it, I had to ask.

"Of course, he does. Red is his favorite color." He winks before walking away.

I'm left standing there alone in this massive home. Red is his favorite color. Red for *The Red Society*. I should have known.

27

CHARLA

Burns walked out the front door over an hour ago and he hasn't returned since. I've roamed the house. Up the stairs, down the stairs. Each time I let my hands run along the banister while trying to picture East here. I must say whoever cleans this place polishes the banister. Smooth like butter.

I've snooped the living room, the sitting area, and even the kitchen. Just to see if I could get any insight into the dark and mysterious man who kindly offered me a place to stay.

I'm still in shock at my father could be so cold. So heartless. Does he even love me, his only child?

Now back in my room, all I do is pace. I keep checking the windows for any sign of life. I haven't even seen a housekeeper.

I stare out the west window at the sun that's now setting. It paints a beautiful pink and orange glow above the trees. Another vast difference from my view. I see the sunrise and East sees the sunset. Both different, yet similar.

I see the beginning of each day and East sees the end. I am the day, and he is the night.

I wonder where East is. He hasn't texted or called at all since leaving me alone with my father. That was such a shit show. My father demanded that I not go with him. That he would cut off my monthly allowance. Like that is going to punish me. I make my own money. Damn good money too. I should text Spencer an update in case he tries to go to my place.

After sending a quick text to my best friend, my thoughts immediately go back to East. Will he even come home tonight? Probably not with it being a Friday and the weekend kicking off. He lives at the club. If he does return, he'll most likely arrive way late.

A bad idea comes to mind, and before I can talk myself out of it, I'm already walking out of my room and headed to the one place I was advised against going to.

His side.

Curiosity gets to me. Why is he so secretive? What is he hiding over there behind the doors? I can't for the life of me figure out why that entire side is cloaked in darkness. Blackout curtains, not a single light on.

Crossing over the threshold, my nerves kick up a notch. There's something thrilling about doing something that I shouldn't be doing. Like East for example. He's the forbidden apple that I can't help but taste over and over, knowing his apple is poisoning me slowly.

I stop at the first door, my hand lands on the knob. I don't even hesitate, opening the door slowly. The room is dark, very dark.

I reach over for the light switch, hit it, and nothing happens. That's odd and a little creepy. I walk in a little to allow my eyes to adjust in the dark. I can barely make out what looks like stacks of magazines. A room of magazines. I laugh. I bet they are *men's* magazines with lots of women posing in nothing. I'd also bet they were probably East's grandfather's since magazines are a thing of the past these days. Why he still has them is beyond me.

I make my way back out to the hall, closing the door behind me. I eye the next door across the hall and those excited flutters take flight again. I head straight for it.

The second my hand touches the knob a throat clears from somewhere behind me. "I wouldn't turn that if I were you."

I jump.

East.

Shit. I've been caught snooping. I turn toward his voice. I can hardly see his silhouette. I can't even make out his face to gauge if he is angry or not.

I drop my hand. "I was bored."

"Burns told you this wing was off limits."

"He did." The last thing I want to do is bring the old man down for my disobedience. "I just chose not to listen."

East slowly walks until is standing directly in front of me. "You seem to have a problem with listening." He nearly spits the words at me.

Shrugging my shoulders, I smile. "Guess you could say that."

He grabs my wrist so fast I didn't see it coming. His grip is tight. Really tight. I hate admitting that it excites me.

I attempt to resist him as he pulls me back into the light, continuing until we are standing in front of my room. Well, the one I'm staying in.

"I gave you the room with the best view, Charla. Don't let me find you over on that side again. Do you understand?"

I say nothing, instead, I turn away, ignoring his demands.

"Damn it, Charla! Stop acting like a child! Tell me you understand!" East is nearly yelling now.

I nod even though I feel like I'm being reprimanded. It pisses me off slightly. "Yes, Father, I understand." I roll my eyes in annoyance.

East drops my hand and grabs my chin roughly, forcing me to meet his eyes. Anger mixed with something I can't quite put my finger on flashes before me.

"I will never be your father. Am I clear on that? Never. I would never treat you the way that man does. I may devour your body, but never would I hurt you the way he has." East is beyond angry. I don't think I've ever seen him this heated.

Holy shit. I swallow slowly. East's eyes never leave mine. He continues staring at me with a hard expression. He's waiting for me to confirm what he just stated. I understand. Loud and clear. So loud heat floods my face and elsewhere.

"I'm glad you're not my father."

At my words, he comes in closer. His lips never touch mine, no instead he bites my jaw line, nipping a trail down to my neck. He bites me hard before sucking. Pain laced with pleasure. The sensation alone has me growing wet. I should be ashamed that it turns me on instantly.

I'm not, though, and I want more.

When he releases his mouth, I already know there will be a mark. I can feel it. The blood rising.

He steps back. "I'm not good for you, but I can't seem to get you to realize that." He takes another step back.

I feel cold at the loss of his touch. He may think he's not good enough for me, however, if he's what I want, then that's all that should matter. Honestly, I'm sick of hearing him say that. I'm sick of tiptoeing around the subject of us. I step into him and place my hand on his chest. The look on his face is priceless. I think I've shocked him.

"See, you should stop saying that. You sound like my father telling me what's good for me." I lean up and kiss his cheek lightly before whipping my hair over my shoulder. Without looking back, I walk into the room he's allowing me to stay in and shut the door behind me.

Two can play this game... I think.

28

What in the hell just happened? Charla just handed me a dose of my own fucking poison, and I swallowed it without having a chance to think twice. Slapped me right in the face. What the fuck? I'm damn impressed. That blonde is growing a backbone. It's sexy as hell too. So sexy my dick twitches against my zipper, wanting to be set free.

I can't though, especially while she is staying here temporarily. I need to get myself together, I never lose control, yet somehow, she has me doing shit I've never done before. I don't understand it, can't explain it.

I walk into my room and shut the door, locking it behind me. I don't put it past that woman to just walk on in without permission just to defy me. I think she gets off by pissing me off.

Sitting on my bed, I grab my hard-on that has yet to go down. It has me realizing that Charla is a dangerous woman. She has no idea either. I crave her when I know I shouldn't. I fuck her knowing I shouldn't.

My dick twitches in my hand.

FUCK!

I'm in trouble. I jump off the bed and leave my room. I know where I'm going. It's a terrible idea, yet I can't seem to stop myself. Can't seem to care. I need a release and there's only one woman lately who gives me the release I crave.

I don't even bother knocking as I barge in. Hell, it is my house anyway. When I enter, I expected her to be sitting on the bed. She's not. Did she fucking leave? I will the blood coursing through my veins to calm down. I listen for a second.

I hear the shower. Something like relief washes over me. It confuses me. I notice the clothes on the floor. I walk to the ensuite bathroom. I open the door quietly and I'm completely blown away by the sight in front of me.

Charla stands in front of me facing the mirror, naked. Her hands rest on the counter. Perfect tits and ass on display for me. So damn sexy. That's not what guts me though.

Her eyes are closed as mascara-filled tears run down her face. The black streaks run all the way down, dripping off her chin and landing on the counter.

For some reason, seeing Charla so broken makes me want to both comfort and fuck her. That's a stupid idea and while I fight with my mind, I just stare at her. Taking every inch of her in.

Any other man would give her space, but not me. I'm not like most men. I take what I want. And right now I want her in the worst way. I want Charla in all her broken, beautiful glory. I want her lips that taste like sweet poison to claim me.

Her eyes open to find me staring at her. The mirror is

starting to fog, but I know she can see the fire in my eyes. It's crystal clear. I want her.

She says nothing as I unbutton my shirt and toss it aside. I unlace my boots next, quickly removing them followed by my socks. I glance back up at Charla. She is still watching through the tiny bit of mirror that hasn't fogged over yet. I keep my eyes trained on hers as I slowly remove my belt. Next goes my slacks and briefs.

I catch a glimpse, watching as her eyes drop to my cock just before the last bit of mirror is covered.

With the belt still in my hand, I step up to her, letting my dick nudge her ass. She pushes back into it.

Fuck.

I set the belt on the counter and reach my hand up to her face. I wipe her black tears across her chin. She continues pushing against me. A slow form of torture. All I want to do is plunge into her pussy. Just not yet. I want to savor Charla like this. She is beautiful with a dark side. A dark side that I can't seem to get enough of. She truly is a form of poison.

"Why are you crying, Charla?"

Her eyes meet mine in the mirror. Those emeralds stare, unblinking. "I'm tired, East. Tired of being controlled. Tired of being told what to do. For once I want to make my own decisions without someone telling me what's best for me."

As if she can't surprise me any more than she already has, she turns, grabbing my cock. Her smooth hand strokes me as she drops to her knees. Her puffy lips envelop me slowly. It's painful holding back when all I want to do is thrust deep into her mouth. I want to make her gag. I want to thrust hard, causing the back of her head to hit the cabinet. I don't. I'm too entranced by the sight below me. Charla on her knees, taking me in her mouth effortlessly while her face is still streaked in mascara while looking up at me.

Fuck, she is a sight.

This moment right here with her like this, I'll remember for the rest of my days. Even when she is long gone from my life, I know I'll jerk off to the vision of her broken soul sucking my dick.

Yup, there is something wrong with me.

I let her continue her rapid movements of milking my cock until I start to feel my balls tighten.

I pull her up by her blonde hair roughly, she whimpers. When I blow my load, I want it to be inside of her. I want her to feel my cum. I want to see it drip out of her and down her thighs. I want her to feel dirty after I've fucked her hard.

Call me a sadist. I don't care. I know she likes it rough.

She doesn't even question when I yank her up. I lean in, biting her neck hard. Her gasps tell me it turns her on. Just to be sure, I cup her pussy hard as I push a finger through her slick folds. She's soaked. Just like I knew she would be.

"So fucking hot for me," I whisper into her neck.

When I pull my finger out of her, she whimpers again. She watches as I bring my finger to my mouth and taste her juices. I swear nothing tastes as good as Charla. Sweet, sweet poison. Her eyes dilate watching me tease her. The second my finger is clean and not an ounce of her is left on it, I grab the belt. She eyes it without fear. I'm pretty certain it's lust I see in her eyes. I spin her around to face the mirror. She braces her hands on the counter as if she already knows what I'm about to do. God, it makes my cock jump. I suddenly want to watch her as I take the belt to her ass.

Quickly grabbing a hand towel, I swipe it across the

mirror. Her eyes find me as I drop the towel. I see it. The desire in them.

I bend her forward a little more. I want the perfect angle.

"I'm going to punish you now."

She stays silent.

I reach back and whip the belt across her left ass cheek. Not too hard, just hard enough to sting. I need to see how she reacts before hitting her ass as hard as I dream of doing.

She yelps, and it causes my dick to twitch. I rub circles over the red mark. She pushes into my hand.

"That was for venturing where you don't belong."

Again, she says nothing.

I slap her right cheek, harder this time. She cries out, and I see her eyes glisten with new tears. I do the same to this cheek. I rub and massage where I hit her with the belt.

"That was for comparing me to your father. I. Am. Not. Your. Father."

"Are you going to fuck me now?"

Her words come out of nowhere. I'm not expecting them. I pull her hair gently to me. She arches exposing her neck for me while her ass rubs against my cock.

I whisper into her ear, "Do you want me to fuck you, Charla?"

"Yes,"

"I won't be gentle."

"You're never gentle."

She has a point. I nip under her ear before releasing her hair. I take the belt and wrap it around both wrists, pulling it tight. I don't want her touching me. When she touches me, it makes me feel shit. Shit I don't need to fucking feel.

Once her wrists are secure, I dip my fingers back

between her legs, I stretch her wet pussy. Her moans tell me this is exactly what she wants.

Pulling my fingers out, I press a hand to her back, pushing her further on the counter and line myself up. I don't even give her or myself time to think. Grabbing her hip with one hand, I thrust right in. Hard. She screams out. I pull back slowly and plunge back into her hard. I continue the same motion repeatedly. It's torture. A slow form of torture I know she craves because she keeps screaming my name. I know my movements will surely cause her to bruise. The way my fingers dig into her hips, the way her body pounds against the counter. I don't let up. I love making her feel pain.

I'm so close, with each slow movement I have to resist. I need her to come undone first.

Reaching around with my other hand, I toy with her clit, pinching, rubbing. Her pussy tightens and it all but sends me over the edge. I still while in her.

"East, move... please." Her moans go straight to my dick. It twitches as her walls tighten even more. The fact that she can't touch me makes this even hotter. Her tied hands grip the counter as much as the belt will allow, which isn't much.

I speed up my circular motions. "Come for me," I demand as I slowly draw back until just the tip is in.

"East!" she screams as I dive in hard. It's her undoing. Hell, it's my undoing too. She comes so fucking hard while screaming my name. I follow directly behind. Filling her with my cum. Just like I pictured. My dick continues jutting, as her pussy milks every last drop of me. Both of us out of breath, panting hard.

Fuck, that was by far the best sex I've ever had.

When I finally pull out of her, she sighs. She looks

content standing there, still gripping the counter firmly. I undo the belt and guide her to the shower. Her legs are weak, she nearly stumbles and I have to keep a hold of her elbow to keep her upright.

We stand under the hot spray of water, saying nothing. Her neck is marked up from me. There are marks on her hips, her ass, and her neck. I'm sure there's bruising between her legs. Something like pride swells in my chest when I look at her body, knowing I did that to her and that she wanted it.

Charla Krauss is mine.

Fuck. What am I thinking?

Just the thought of my marks on her body has me wanting to sink back into her again, claiming her again and again until she can't walk.

These thoughts are ludicrous. Making her mine was never part of the plan.

Plans change, I tell myself as I grab a cloth to clean the woman standing in front of me.

29

CHARLA

It took a shit load of concealer and even more foundation to cover my neck this morning. The marks East left on me would look trashy to anyone who took one look at them. For me, though, they are a reminder of how raw last night was. East caught me in what could be considered one of my absolute lowest points. Anger and hurt consumed me and I finally gave into the tears. I didn't expect East to walk in on me to witness me at my worst.

But he did.

And boy am I glad he did.

Now, though, I'm squeezing my thighs shut while sitting in my office trying to concentrate. I'm sore and all I can think of is the sound of the belt across my ass. How bad it stung, how good it felt when his strong hands rubbed the spot he hit. There must be something wrong with me. I'm turned on just replaying what happened. We didn't even speak afterward. He guided me into the shower and washed my body, being extra careful between my legs and ass.

I won't lie and say it didn't do things to my heart

because it did. My stupid heart wants to feel something for East. So not a good idea. He probably fucks multiple women daily. Just the thought has me remembering when I walked in on him and one of the strippers. Shaking my head, I realize that he is not a one-woman kind of guy. He didn't even speak this morning when Burns drove us back into the city for work. He didn't even say goodbye when I got out of the dark car, he didn't even glance up from his phone. These are just reminders that while the sex is amazing. He is not.

"So, how was your first night with him?" Spencer asks, standing in the doorway to my office.

I didn't even hear him come in.

"It was…" I bite my lip, trying to come up with a quick lie because there is no way I'm telling my best guy friend that East bent me over the bathroom counter, took a belt to my ass, and then fucked me senseless.

Nope, no way.

"That good, huh?"

"It was fine. It'll take some getting used to."

"You know you can always stay with me."

"No, I don't want to cramp your bachelor pad. Besides, East's house is huge. He stays on his side. It'll be fine."

That's most definitely a lie because if incidents like last night continue to happen, things will not be fine.

"All right, but the offer stands. If he becomes an asshole, you leave and come straight to me."

"Of course. You know I'm not putting up with any more control, Spence."

"Right. Do you realize that you don't even have your Lexus? He is having his driver take you everywhere. That's control. You know that, right?"

He has a point. I had forgotten all about my vehicle

until just now. "I'll be getting my car. He just offered to get me out of there fast because of my father."

Spencer says nothing, just rubs his chin. He's silently assessing me. His eyes roam me, squinting here and there. I don't like it. I hate being judged. I get that shit enough.

"Stop staring at me like that," I snap, standing quickly. He may be my best friend, but I will not have him judging me.

He puts his hands up in surrender. "Hey, calm down. I'm just worried about you." He pushes off the door frame and walks away leaving me standing there, frustrated.

How is this my life? It's the magical question I keep asking myself.

Upon leaving work, I asked East's driver to take me to my condo so that I could get a few things and my vehicle. He didn't want to at first, stating that East would be upset. However, I held my ground. I told him if he didn't take me there, I would call a cab and go there. Either way, I was going to my place. I wanted my sexy beast; I refuse to be controlled or trapped as Spencer pointed out.

Burns complied which earned me a nasty text from the bad boy himself. I just chose to ignore it.

I, Charla Krauss, am finding my voice. I'm finding myself and I don't care who I piss off in the making.

———

I've been at East's for exactly one week. It's been pretty quiet. He comes home super late, and we don't speak. I think he's avoiding me. I eat alone and then retreat to my room. It's lonely and I'm growing annoyed with the silence that only seems to be growing between us.

I almost invited Spencer to come over for dinner tonight

yet couldn't bring myself to hit send on the text. Nope, I deleted it and powered off my phone. There's something about keeping East's mansion private. I don't want to share it with anyone. What happens between these walls is for only us. So I'd like to think anyway.

My father has called every single day and every single day I hit the ignore button. He never leaves a voicemail. Instead, he then texts telling me I need to stop acting foolishly and that I'm embarrassing him. I want to tell him he is the one acting crazy and that he's only embarrassing himself. I don't. It's pointless. He never listens anyway.

After his calls and texts come Corey's. He does the exact same as my father, calls first, doesn't leave a voicemail, and then texts me that I need to grow up. Fuck him and all his bullshit that got me into this damn mess to begin with.

Every now and then negative thoughts try to creep in. Would life be easier with Corey? I'd have everything in a materialistic sense, but I'd feel nothing. I would be an empty shell of myself. Being with Corey would mean being miserable. No, thanks.

I even thought about running to the damn paparazzi to tell them just what their mayor has done to his only daughter; however, just the thought of speaking with any of them makes my skin crawl. Plus, I've been in the limelight enough with that intimate photo of East and I.

So I just stay quiet and wish for a different tomorrow.

30

CHARLA

I'm nose deep in numbers when Spencer comes barging into my office.

"Charla! You need to see this!" He's rushed in so fast a trail of fire couldn't even keep up with him.

"Not now, Spence, I'm in the middle of this account." I wave him off going back to what I was doing.

He's not hearing me, though, because he slams a hand on my desk, causing me to jump.

"Fuck that account, Charla. Shit is going to go down. You need to read this!" His loud voice vibrates through my veins and the shiver that climbs my spine tells me something bad has happened. Which sucks because life has been so quiet.

"Jesus, Spence, what is it?"

He shoves his phone in my face. I snatch it and start reading. I feel the color drain from my face as I read the words.

What is this?

MOTHER OF EAST SINCLAIR, OWNER OF THE RED SOCIETY, BEING
RELEASED EARLY NEXT WEEK AFTER SERVING ALMOST TWENTY YEARS
FOR CHILD ABUSE.

I continue reading. Horrible recaps of East's childhood. The descriptive words have me in tears. How could a mother be so harsh to her child? Spencer comes to stand behind me, putting a hand on my shoulder. Probably to help the shakes that are starting to rack my body. I'm in shock as I read on.

No.

Oh my god.

East's past life is being dug up and thrown back into the limelight.

The comments are brutal. Keyboard warriors don't hold back.

"It's only fitting he runs a strip joint, he was raised in a strip club because mommy was too busy neglecting him. He has to get attention somewhere"
"No wonder he's screwed up enough to run a strip club. Mom locked him up, starved him, and beat him."

I slide the phone away and the tears start to fall. I can't read anymore. His mother is a monster. No wonder he's never once spoken of her.

"Charla, this is going to blow up. I think you need to stay at my place until this blows over. You don't know how Sinclair is going to act."

"What? No. If anything, he's going to need someone."

Before I realize what I'm doing, I send him a text.

Are you okay?

Not now Charla

I've seen the news. I know.

Of course, you have

Are you at the club?

I don't need you coming here. I don't need
saving

Too bad, I'm already on my way.

I'm up and grabbing my things before my mind can even catch up.

"Char, wait... I'm serious. You don't know what can of worms and past trauma has just been opened up. You could be walking into a ticking time bomb, and I don't think it's safe." Spencer grabs my upper arm gently, which causes me to pause and turn to him.

"I'm not scared of East. He won't hurt me." I've never been so certain of anything before. I feel it though. East will not hurt me. He won't.

"I don't trust him."

I smile at my friend. "I know you don't. But I do."

Reluctantly, Spencer finally releases me, and I jet out of my office so fast that the people I pass are a complete blur.

Everything is a blur until I pull up and put my SUV in park in front of The Red Society. I look around, there are news vans and reporters parked all over.

Shit. This is really bad.

I'm grateful for my dark tint because a few of the snakes have glanced my way. I quickly throw it in reverse and drive around to the backside. There's a man outside the back door, I sort of recognize him as I park. I think he's the guy who let me in before.

"Where's East?"

"Ma'am, I'm not at liberty to discuss. You need to leave."

"He is expecting me."

"He's not expect— " The big dude is cut off by that deep voice that I've come to know well.

"Charla, I told you not to come." His hard eyes land on me. Zero emotion on his face. It makes my heart ache.

"I needed to make sure you were okay."

"I'm fine. Go home. I'll be there within the hour."

"But— "

"No buts, go home now. Before someone sees you and decides to follow you."

I nod, he has a point. The last thing either of us needs

is more attention. I walk back to my car, taking one last glance at the dark man. I know now, deep down, that he is broken. That's why he's closed off. His mother broke him.

My father broke me with cruel words. East's mother broke him physically and that's way worse than anything my father has ever done. My heart breaks for him.

The entire way home, I shed tears. I can't for the life of me comprehend how a parent can physically harm their child. Just why? I know it's pointless to ask myself these questions. No answers will ever justify such a thing.

I watch from the window in the sitting area as East pulls up. Just like he said, he arrived home in less than an hour. I'm grateful because I kept looking up articles and that was the worst thing to do. Lots of archives came up, revealing just how horrible East's abuse was at the hands of his mother. Then came the blasting of how his grandfather could raise a boy in a strip club. That he was bound to turn out to be a disgusting man looking at naked chicks all day and night.

Such horrible articles were published. So bad that East's grandfather, Archer Sinclair, pulled East from public school and enrolled him in a private school. He wasn't allowed to be filmed or any photos published.

I give his grandfather credit. It seems he did all he could to make sure East grew up with as normal a life as possible.

I'm standing by the door as he enters. The minute he shuts it, his broken eyes find mine. I rush to him.

"East, I'm sorry— "

I don't get to finish speaking because he grabs the back of my neck, yanking me into him. His lips crush mine. Shock runs through me. He never kisses me. He hates it. His kiss is hard, he forces my mouth open with his tongue taking what he wants. Needing to control something and I let him. He needs this.

He pours everything he is feeling into our kiss. The hurt, the hate, even the humiliation he feels. I feel it all straight down to my toes. I tear at his shirt, popping buttons as I go. My hands go to roam his chest and he instantly grabs them, pulling them behind my back. It clicks then. He doesn't like to be touched. It's because of his mother. The ache in my chest only grows. I break our kiss, pulling back. Both of us totally out of breath.

"Let me touch you, East. Please."

"No."

"Please."

"You don't understand, can't understand."

"You're right, I can't, but I won't hurt you."

It's the honest truth. I don't understand. I can't begin to understand what he has endured. What I can understand is the need to try to fix him, to touch him, and replace the hurt.

East rests his head against mine, his breathing is still erratic. "Don't you see, you do have the power to hurt me."

I pull back at his words. He's opening up. The pain etched across his face nearly kills me. I want so badly to reach out and touch him, I can't though because he still has my hands behind my back.

"East, I'm here. I'm not going anywhere." I step in and kiss him. I kiss him slowly until he opens back up. It's hard not being able to touch him. Yet I'm determined to kiss him with all I have. He needs to feel what I feel when we are together. He has to feel it. I know he does. He's just scared. In a way, I'm scared too, yet I continue kissing him until I finally feel him relax his grip slightly. I take his moment of weakness and pull my hands free, grabbing his opened shirt, to pull him even closer. I'm careful not to run my hands against his skin. I hold the material in a death grip while pouring myself into him.

We pull apart, gasping for air. He grips me under my ass and yanks me up into his arms. On instinct, I wrap my legs around him. I can feel his erection through my thin work slacks. He carries me over to the couch and sets me down before enveloping me with his strong body. I nuzzle into his neck, kissing and nipping. The scent of his cologne has me yanking his shirt off. He surprises me by letting me. I pull my navy blouse over my head. East takes over, freeing my breasts from my lace bra. He sucks and bites, sending electricity straight to my core. I can't help but grind into him.

Suddenly he pulls back. Steps away abruptly.

"No, Charla. Not like this. I'm not fucking you like this. I don't need guilt sex."

"What?" His harsh words come as a surprise. This isn't because I feel bad for him. I mean, yeah, I feel bad about his childhood, but that's not the reason for this. I wanted to give him control.

He throws my top at me. "Put that back on."

"This isn't about guilt, East. I wanted you. I thought I made that loud and clear. I was giving you complete control over me." I stand, holding my blouse in my hand.

"That's a stupid thing to do. Don't give me control, Charla. That would be a dangerous game to play with me."

I step right up in his face. "Stop telling me what to do. I want to give you control. Fucking take it."

My words cause him to snap. East tosses me over his shoulder harshly and carries me up the stairs.

31

EAST

Her words slice through me. They are my undoing. How the fuck she manages to get under my skin is beyond me. I shouldn't have kissed her. Shouldn't have caved. No woman should have that kind of control over me. I don't do love or any of that kissing shit. What is she doing to me? After having a woman harm me with her hands, I swore off letting any woman touch me. Swore off letting love poison me.

Walking into her room, I toss her ass on the bed and climb on over her, keeping my arms extended by each side of her face. She's panting already, excited for what is to come. I wish she feared me. Instead, I only turn her on, bringing out a side of her only I knows exists. I kind of like that I am the only one who gets this version of Charla.

Grabbing her throat slightly, her breath hitches. "You still want to give me control?" I ask as I squeeze a little tighter. Maybe if I scare her, she'll rethink this. Secretly, in the back of my mind, I hope she doesn't though. There's no one who lets me do the things I do to her.

Her eyes focus on mine. Unblinking. "Take control, East.

I can handle it." Her words are confident, even with restricted air supply. Just the thought makes my dick twitch. I release her neck and look for the red marks I've put there. Where are the marks from the other night? They couldn't have faded already. I rub the spots where I know I left them.

Makeup.

I step back off the bed and go into the bathroom. When I return with the damp cloth, I wipe her neck clean. I want to see my marks. Call me sick, it is what it is. The bruising has faded a little; still, seeing them with the new marks I've just added turns me on further.

I begin removing my clothes in a haste. She makes to remove her bra and I stop her.

"Don't fucking move."

She sinks back on the bed and watches me. She eyes my cock that finally springs free as I push my boxer briefs down. I can't wait to sink into her wet pussy. Yet I don't want to rush this. I undo her pants and yank them down, leaving her black panties on. Rubbing my dick over her center through them causes her to arch into me. I pinch a nipple through the lace.

"East," she moans, continuing to grind into me. I run my fingers down her body lightly before pulling the thin black material to the side. I push a finger through her slick folds. I love how wet she is for this. For me. Inserting a second finger causes her to grab at my hair. Dammit.

Her touch does things to me. Things I'm unsure of.

"Look at me, Charla," I demand as I pull two fingers out and bring them to my lips. Her lust-filled gaze follows my fingers as I pull them into my mouth to suck her juices off. I don't miss when she swallows hard.

"You taste like a drug I can't get enough of. The perfect

drug."

"Is this okay?" she asks as her hands go to touch my chest. I freeze for a split second before nodding, finally letting her touch me. So much me holding all control.

And hell, if her hands aren't the softest things ever as they explore every ridge. I'm tense but it's not because of what she is doing. It's because I'm not used to it. It's a foreign feeling. It feels good though. So good that I reach down and pull her panties hard, ripping them off of her.

I waste no time driving my dick into her wet pussy. She screams out and grabs at my chest. It only drives me into her harder. She moans my name and it's the sweetest fucking sound. She wraps her arms around my neck and pulls me to her mouth.

I hesitate.

Kissing while fucking is a huge red flag. A big no no. So why am I fucking opening my mouth to kiss her back? Why am I allowing our tongues to dance as I fuck her harder than I ever have? The moans vibrating between us cloud all thoughts. I can't tell whose moans are whose. Everything is hazy.

The minute I feel her tightening, I pull back to watch her. I want to see her lose control, to surrender completely to me. I yank her hips up slightly, causing her to wrap her legs around me. Her eyes flutter close and I know I've hit her sweet spot. I fuck her with everything I have and when she comes, she comes hard, screaming out my name while grabbing my arms, her red nails digging in will leave a mark. Just the thought of her marking my body like she owns me has me spilling into her. I don't stop until she's milked every ounce of cum from my throbbing dick.

I collapse on top of her, both of us covered in a sheen of sweat, panting. She opens her eyes and runs a hand down my face, caressing me. We stay quiet for a moment. What just happened between us? I don't kiss. I don't allow women to ever touch me. Somehow this blonde is slowly breaking down the barrier I built up after I was free of my mother.

"What are you doing to me?" I whisper across her fingers that are tracing my lips.

"I don't know, but I think I like it."

"We are wrong for each other." It's the truth. We are.

"Says who?" she asks as she slides out from under me. She nudges me to roll onto my back. She straddles me. I can't help but look down to see the white substance dripping out of her. Knowing I put it there has this primal feeling coursing through my veins. My dick jumps.

Charla runs her hands all over me. "Thank you... for letting me touch you." She comes down, kissing my lips again. In one quick motion, she slides down on my cock. Her hair falls as she arches her back, riding me.

It is hands down the hottest thing I have ever witnessed. And I've seen a lot, being the owner of a strip club.

Charla takes control, her body moving effortlessly on top of mine. Reaching up, I pinch both nipples. It sends her over the edge as she chases her release. My eyes are glued to where our bodies meet. A mixture of both of us drips out of her cunt. She starts to collapse on top of me, but I'm fast and roll over back over not wasting a minute before diving back into her, fucking her hard all over again. I may have given her control for a little bit, but now it's time to remind her that I am in control. I pull her blonde hair back, giving me perfect access to her neck.

Charla is a drug. Her body is addicting. I won't become addicted. The promise of a lie. I tell it to myself anyway.

32

CHARLA

After another round of the most amazing sex ever, East ran me a bath. He didn't get in with me, though he washed me. He left a towel and a robe before stepping out. He wasn't in the room when I came out, so I assumed he needed some space. I needed some time to breathe myself. It left me relaying our night over and over until I gave into sleep.

What we did was rough, dirty. What's more, East let me touch him. He let me kiss him. It was a shock to my soul. The sweetest shock. As much as I try to fight this feeling that has started creeping into my heart, I fear if I stay here much longer while continuing whatever this is with him, I may fall hard. That thought alone scares me.

Shaking this feeling, I head out for coffee. I slept longer than I anticipated, and I need to get moving. Each step is a reminder of last night. I'm sore.

The minute I open my door, his scent invades my nostrils. It's as if he was just standing outside of my door. Maybe he was. I don't know.

I continue down the stairs to see the coffee has

already been made, a cup set out next to the pot for me. Red, of course. I grab it and pour myself a cup. It's silent in this large house. Too quiet, so I wander out back and sit near the pool. A black bottom pool. It's huge. A rectangle. Perfect for doing laps. I think after work today, I'll swim. I didn't pack my suit, not that it matters. I'm usually alone until way late. A little skinny dipping won't be a big deal.

After two cups of coffee, I get dressed and check in with Spencer. He told me I was good to work from home as long as I send him over the financial report I was working on before the day's end. That won't be hard since I was nearly finished with it when I rushed out yesterday. Spencer is still insisting that I stay with him. I told him I was fine and that we would do lunch tomorrow. He wasn't too happy but agreed to lunch.

———

Emails have been sent over to Spencer. Grabbing a towel, I head back out to the pool. I strip, not bothering to look around. No need to. This place is secluded. After laying my clothes on the lounge chair, I pull my hair down and head toward the water. Dipping my toes in the dark water, it feels good. Almost the right temperature. I dive in.

There's something eerie about swimming in a black bottom pool. It's dark. Another thing to remind me that East has a dark soul to match his bad boy attitude. I wipe the wet hair from my face and start doing laps. The water is almost soothing. My sore muscles welcome it.

I'm winded from a few laps. It's been a while since doing that type of workout. I get out and take a sip of water. The sun is starting to set. I hope the lights surrounding the pool are set up on a timer. I am not sure I have it in me to search for a switch somewhere.

Walking back to the edge of the deep end, I dive in once again, headed for the shallow end with plans to just float around. Those plans quickly change when I come up for air to find East standing at the edge. Staring.

And holy shit, can the man get any hotter?

He stands there, eyes locked on me, wearing black dress slacks, and a dress shirt to match with a red tie that's been loosened. His hands are casually in his front pockets. Hair slicked back. God, he's so fucking hot.

"You're swimming." His words come out as a statement.

"I am. I didn't expect you to be here so early."

"Surprise." He smirks.

"Join me?"

"No." Again, another statement.

Once my feet find the bottom, I stand up straighter, my naked upper half on full display for East's haunting eyes. They haunt me every night. The way his eyes gaze over my body, it does something to me. It's as if he can light a match the next time he blinks, setting my body on fire.

"Like what you see?"

I swim to the edge of the pool where he stands. The minute I come close, he squats down. Deciding to tease the man who brings me to delicious highs, I prop my elbows up on the side. It pushes my breasts together, water dripping down them. The cool evening air causes my nipples to harden. Looking at the bulge that is evident in East's pants, it is clear that he likes what he sees. Lust fills his eyes, igniting the match. Sending the flames straight down my spine.

"Charla." His deep voice is strained. I love what I do to him almost as much as I love what he does to my body.

I reach out with one hand wondering if he'll let my wet hands touch him through his clothes.

He does.

East lets out a low growl and it makes me want more. It gives me a wild idea. Popping up out of the water further, I pull his zipper down, grab his cock, and pull it free.

The minute I begin stroking him ever so slowly, he drops from a squat to his knees. His erection even with my face. Licking my lips once, my mouth encircles just the tip. It drives him mad. Quiet curses leave his lips as I take him deeper. I keep a slow and steady motion until his hand fists my hair forcing me to take him faster.

My eyes water and the urge to gag is strong as he keeps pumping into my mouth deeper. Even still, I want it. I feel alive when East is rough with me. The way he uses my mouth to take what he wants from me, well, it turns me on to the point I'm itching for more while resisting the impulse to grind on the damn edge of the pool.

It's not long before salty spurts of cum hit the back of my throat. East pulls back, adjusting himself. Without warning he grabs my arm, yanking me out of the dark water, causing me to yelp.

There I stand, wet and completely naked in front of East Sinclair.

"Skinny dipping in my pool," he grits.

Is he mad? No, there's no way. "I wanted to go for a swim and I didn't pack any of my suits."

"You should have allowed me to send the movers there to collect your things."

He's right, I probably should have said yes when he asked, however, I was hoping my oh-so-wonderful father would have called by now to tell me I can come home. That hasn't happened and so here I am naked.

"Are you complaining, Mr. Sinclair?"

East shakes his head. "Always surprising me." He flashes a wicked smile as he continues dragging me over to the pool bar that is tucked away in the corner. I didn't even know he had one. By the way the plants and shrubs surround it, you'd never know it was there.

The sun has since gone down, and the lights cast a glow around the patio. The bar is dark though. East stops in front of it and walks around to flip on a switch. Low lights come on from above. Is there nothing bright about this man? Everything is dark with East. I like it that way though.

He comes back around and hoists me up on the bar. The cold granite makes me squirm, but he grips my hips, keeping me firmly in place. I watch as he removes one hand to push me down on my back. The cold that surges through me is promptly forgotten the minute East bites the inside of my thigh. After he bites, he sucks on the spot. He does the exact same thing to my other thigh.

"Marking you is a drug to me." His hooded eyes peer up from between my legs.

I raise an eyebrow, unable to form words. The fire that runs through my body is hot and I'm burning for more. More of East's mouth, his hands. I want all of him even if he eventually puts the fire out, leaving me forever scarred. At least I'll be able to say I felt alive.

He keeps biting and sucking. I'm fighting to control my rapid breathing. How have I been living before East?

I haven't, I've just been existing.

"Do you like when I mark you, Charla?"

I nod.

"Say it."

"Yes, I like when you mark me."

His eyes stay on mine as his mouth comes down, biting

me in my most sensitive parts. The sensation results in me calling out his name while my hands fly to his hair, forcing him to stay there. I watch as he fucks my mouth with his tongue.

East winks at me. Actually winks as his tongue starts on my clit. He teases me, licking and sucking. After a minute his fingers are on me, dipping in easily, all the while keeping his mouth exactly where I need it to be. Just when I think I won't last much longer, East removes his fingers from my pussy. Suddenly I feel them dancing over my ass then between my crack. I freeze.

"Relax, Charla."

I'm not sure how I feel about this. No one has ever touched me there. His fingers, wet from my juices, rub the tight spot.

"Just breathe." His husky voice vibrates over my bud, causing a heated sensation to run through my body. He senses it and uses the moment to push a finger through. I cry out, but it's soon replaced with pleasure. A different kind of pleasure I have yet to experience. His tongue is back on me. I can't take it. Squeezing my eyes shut, I allow East to push me right over the edge. No questions asked. I lose myself to the things he does to my body. It's pure bliss. Pure pleasure.

As soon as my shaking subsides, East pulls away, leaving me feeling empty. "You can go back to swimming now." He straightens and walks away toward his massive house.

I open my mouth to say something, anything. No words come. Instead, I lay there naked and splayed out on East's pool bar like he didn't just feast on my pussy before walking off.

33

CHARLA

I woke up early and decided to go straight to work. Spencer is leaning up against my door, two coffees in hand. As much as I want to avoid this conversation and stay in the bubble that I'm currently in, I can't. Spencer is my best friend and I know he is just concerned. Knowing how my father and Corey are, he has a right to be.

He straightens, opening the door for me. He follows me in and shuts it quietly.

"Good morning, Spence."

"Charla." He hands me the hot liquid without saying anything more. His eyes do the rest of the talking as they stare at me unblinking.

Why does he keep doing that? I clear my throat to get his attention. I don't need things to be weird between us. Life is stressful enough right now.

"I'm worried about you. I have a terrible suspicion that your father and Corey are up to something."

"What do you mean?" I come around to my side of the desk and sit down, powering on my computer.

"Look at the news. The pap is eating up your boy's past, dragging his name and his club through the mud. You think that was random? You think it was a coincidence that his mom was released early?"

I shrug. Truth be told, I really hadn't thought about why they dug up his past. I assumed the reporters had a field day because she was released. That was it. The way Spencer puts it though, has me second-guessing. He thinks this was planned.

"What are you saying?"

"Nothing." He takes a long sip of his coffee. "I just have a bad feeling that this might have been set up. Something isn't sitting right with me."

"I don't know. Maybe, maybe not. I just wish it would all go away. The photo of me and him, his past stories. I'm so sick of being in the limelight." I am, and I need a damn moment or two to breathe.

"I agree. Sadly, though, unless you give into your father, it's not going to go away. You need to figure out how to handle it. Perhaps staying with me will help some."

He's right. I will not tell him that though. I secretly enjoy staying with East, even if he leaves me alone for long periods of time and is out doing God knows what. The thought of him screwing other women comes to mind. I have to bite back the jealous feeling that washes over me.

"I'll think about it, Spence."

He is staring again.

"Why do you keep staring at me like that?"

"Sorry." He shakes his head and walks out of my office, shutting the door behind him.

The rest of my workday is quiet. I'm left alone to submit reports to Spencer and a few other advisors so they can decide if they will take on the current account I've been working on. They like money and if an account brings them money, they'll do it. This one surely will, but it's still a new and upcoming business. Still, it's a risk.

As I'm shutting my lights to leave for the evening, Spencer stops by. The look on his face tells me he is about to deliver more bad news.

"Charla, I think you need to go get your things from Sinclair. Come straight to my place after."

"What? Why?"

My friend swallows slowly. "Just listen to me for once and do what I tell you."

His firm voice and hard eyes have me worried. He isn't telling me what has happened and that can only mean one thing; shit is about to hit the fan.

"Okay," I whisper, agreeing blindly to Spencer's demand.

"Good, I'll walk you to your car."

Well, fuck. Now I'm really on edge.

When we arrive at my car, Spencer makes me promise on our friendship, like a child, that I will come to his place after packing. I'm afraid to check social media. To avoid it, I power down my phone. I don't think I can handle it anymore. At least not until I'm back at Spencer's where I can hide away. The whole forty-minute drive to East's though, I wonder what could be so bad this time. Can it get worse?

Yes, yes it can.

I know this to be true because the minute my SUV pulls up the long driveway and into the front of the house, I spot East standing on the front steps, hands across his chest looking angrier than I have ever seen him.

I sit there for a minute, afraid to get out. For the first time ever, I am afraid of East. I suddenly wish I had checked my social media or at the very least, asked Spencer to fill me in.

East is down the steps, stalking toward me. I hit the lock button. Something doesn't feel right. Which is confusing because just last night, like so many nights, he devours me. He's been treating me like I'm his. But this feeling right now in my gut, I can't place.

When he pulls on the handle to find it locked, his face reddens. "Open the fucking door, now."

I don't. His angry words have me frozen in place, afraid to make a move.

"Dammit, Charla! Open the door!" His hand slams on the window, causing me to jump. Fuck! Something has happened and it's not good. Not at all. I need to just get this over with. Like the anticipation of ripping off a band-aid.

Stupidly, against my better judgment, I hit the unlock button. In an instant East yanks open my door, pulling me out.

"What the fuck, East?" He's rough and normally I like when he is. But this is different.

"Tell me, you little spoiled bitch, do you enjoy the games you play?"

"What the hell are you talking about?"

"Come on, joke's over. You can run back to Daddy now. After all, I'm sure he is paying you for this." His voice raises at that last bit.

"Excuse me?! I have no idea what the fuck you are talking about, East!" I scream and pull my arm from his tight grip. He releases it and steps back, running his hand through his hair.

"You," he points a finger at me, "have disrupted my life. You and your fucked up father and piece of shit of a to-be husband."

It's like he slapped me across the face. I get that since meeting him, it's been a wild ride. It's been intense, however, I'm not sure I'm following where he is going with this new accusation, so I keep my mouth shut and try to keep it together.

Fury is still very clear across his features as he opens his phone, scrolling to whatever it is he is looking for. When he finds it, his eyes shoot to mine. The way he looks at me, it's something new. Something like disgust stares back. Those dark eyes hate me.

"In a bizarre turn of events, Stefan Krauss, mayor vouches for the early release of Kelly Sinclair." He spits the words out as if it is the most vile thing he's ever said out loud.

I repeat the words in my head, reality crashing into me. My father has done some sneaky things, but this takes the trophy, releasing such a person to get back at East.

The man standing in front of me, the one I've started to develop feelings for, is blaming me like I was in on it the entire time. That doesn't sit well with me and quite frankly, it sort of pisses me off.

"If you think I had a part in this, you need to think again."

"Think? How else would you explain this?" He flicks his thumb on the screen again. "Charla Krauss meets boyfriend's mom." East turns the phone in my direction. There's a photo under the headline. An older woman faces the camera with another whose back is facing the camera. Blonde hair flows down her back. Umm, what in the hell?

My eyes fly to East. He gives me the nastiest look before storming away.

I shake my head. *That's not me, East.*

I've never met his mother. I have absolutely no desire to meet such a person.

But how do I explain that to East?

34

CHARLA

Somehow, I manage to force my feet to move. Spencer was right. I should stay with him. I need to pack my stuff.

Entering the house as quietly as I possibly can, I realize I am far from quiet. I have on heels. Each step through the foyer echoes throughout the quiet home. No way of hiding my presence.

As my heels hit the top step, I catch a glimpse of a dark shadow. Turning toward his wing, I see him standing in the shadows. I don't have to see his face to know he is staring at me. I can feel his eyes burning me. I try to come up with something to say but fall short. What's there to say? Even if I tell him the truth that it isn't me in the photo, how would he believe me? Or better yet, why would he believe me? My father gave her freedom. I'm associated with the enemy.

Feeling defeated, and unable to gain control of this situation, I continue to my room, closing the door behind me. I don't need an audience while packing the few things I have with me. This has been a ridiculous time in my life. I've never been so reckless before.

Shoving shit in my bag, I start to wonder if being with Corey would just be easier. What if I meet someone else? Will my father pull this crazy shit with other men? Am I destined to be controlled forever?

No, hell no. I won't do it. I tell myself while retrieving my toiletries from the bathroom. I can't go back to who I was before. I'll lose myself if I give in to my father's control.

Lost in my thoughts as I walk back out into the room, I find East standing there. He startles me and I drop my toiletry bag. He looks down at it for a split second before his darker-than-night eyes land on mine. Zero emotion across his face.

Whatever. If he wants to be angry without getting facts, that's on him. I grab my bag and continue packing. I do my best to avoid his hard stare. It's hard though. Even with my back to him as I arrange my things, I can feel his heated gaze.

"You're leaving," he says flatly.

"I am."

"Good."

That one word sets me off. "Really, East?" With my hand on my hip, I let my voice be heard. "You have some nerve accusing me. Do you think I would put myself through all this hell if Daddy was paying me? That I would live this hell, pretending with you? Because if so, you are deranged. My father isn't paying me a dime. Go by my condo any time of day, see if there is security standing in front of the door. That's right, my oh-so-amazing father has a guard there to make sure I don't enter. But it's a setup, right?"

I suck in a deep breath, turning back to my bag. I'm not finished with him though. I pull the zipper hard, closing up what contents I do have with me before looking back at the devil.

"What? Did you think I was just letting you use my body like I'm some sort of a whore because I was setting you up? Reality check, I would NEVER let you put your hands on me if I didn't want them on me, and I surely wouldn't allow you to touch me as part of some setup. I'm not that low and if you think I am, you're damn crazy East."

I hoist my bag on my shoulders and go to shove past him. He stops me, grabbing my wrist. He leans in close to my ear. For some stupid reason, hope swells in my chest, thinking he may apologize for jumping the gun. It is quickly shut down when opens his mouth.

"Your father did this. You did this too. Remember, you wanted me to play the role of your fake boyfriend. So yeah, you did this. You act like you are perfect but in reality, you are nothing but a trust fund baby. Now go run back to daddy dearest."

The venom he just spit at me cuts straight to my heart. My father may have done this. I may have unknowingly played a role by involving East. It wasn't intentional, I just wanted Corey and my father to back off. But I'm not some trust fund baby. I make my own damn money.

Yanking my hand out of his grip, I rush away from him, making my way down the stairs as fast as my feet in heels will allow. When I reach the door, I look back one last time to find that asshole standing at the top, looking down on me.

"By the way, that wasn't me in the photo with your mother. Did you stop and think that it could have been another one of your strippers? Probably not, it's easier to blame me. The fact that you thought it was tells me all I need to know about you. You can go to hell."

My parting words cause him to open his mouth, but I don't stick around to listen to what hate he may fire off. I don't want to hear what he has to say. At least that's what I tell myself. My heart wants to fight me on that. My brain tells me no.

Shoving my belongings in the back seat, I hurry and climb into the front, locking the door. There's no telling if he'll come out and try to stop me. Knowing me, I'd unlock the door and allow him to belittle me some more. Nope, not a chance.

The new me will no longer be treated in such a way.

Pulling away, I look through the rearview mirror at his house, his mansion. To my surprise, East is outside, standing in the same place I found him when I pulled up not even an hour ago. A look of shame or maybe regret is written across his face. Part of me wants to turn my SUV around. The other part, well, that part says no way. It's now up to East to fix this shit. If there even is anything to fix. It's not like we were a couple. It is crazy how quickly things between us changed and not for the good. I can't dwell on that right now though. I have bigger issues at hand.

East's reflection starts to blur the further down the drive I go. This is for the best. I need to get shit squared away with my father. I have bigger issues than some silly crush.

I hit speed dial on Spencer to let him know I'm on my way.

Spencer was right. With him is the best place to be right now.

35

EAST

The house feels empty. Quiet. After three days, her scent still lingers and I feel her everywhere. I hate it, yet dare I say I miss her? I shouldn't miss her. I like the quiet. I like my space being my own and I like being alone.

Right now though, I sort of wish Charla was here. I have pent-up aggression over all the bullshit that has been dug up. What I wouldn't give to fuck that blonde senseless right now. Sure, I have my hand, but that won't do. There's only one body I want and that's the one that takes everything I do without question.

Fuck.

Instead, I distract myself with thoughts of the woman who gave birth to me. Her being free sets me off. Kelly. Her name tastes like acid on my tongue. Even after all these years, the hate I harbor for her is strong. Time hasn't allowed the anger to fade. Not even a little bit, and the fact that Charla's father had a part in her release, really pisses me off.

That fucker hit a nerve. What's worse is he probably knew I would take it out on Charla. I shouldn't have let him win. I just couldn't stop the anger seeping through me and when I saw her, well I lost it. I feel bad for taking it all out on her. Too late, though, I couldn't control the rage pumping through my veins. The damage is done, but not entirely. Not if I can help it.

I've been doing some digging on Stefan Krauss. It's going to cost me a pretty penny but once I have records in my hand, it will either confirm my suspicions and open up a scandal bigger than me or it'll just be a damn waste of time and money.

Either way, I am out for revenge, and one way or another I'm going to get it.

———

"Boss."

I look up and see Marc standing in my doorway, envelope in hand. I hope that is what I think it is. Hope swells in my chest.

"Yes, Marc, come in."

"This arrived just now, figured it might be important."

I nod, holding out my hand for him to place the large brown envelope in.

"You've been quiet, is everything okay, with what is going on?"

"Yes." My response is clipped. Everything is not okay, but I'm counting on the contents in this envelope to change all that.

"Has she tried to call anymore?"

He's referring to Kelly. That vile human had balls showing up here a few nights ago. Security denied her entry and the police were called. She was issued a no trespassing warning. After that, the phone calls started.

Mother dearest claims she just wants to apologize and make amends for the past. Fuck that. There's no going back. The things she did to me no child should ever endure.

"No, I had the number she was calling from blocked."

Marc nods, smiling. I can tell he wants to ask more.

Waving my hand for him to continue, I say, "Go on, ask."

"I notice you've been spending more time here and less time with her."

The way he says *her* causes me to grind my teeth. Is it that noticeable? I only nod, unsure of what to say. I mean I guess I could say that I snapped blaming her for her father's bullshit and accused her of being in that photo and my accusations sent her away.

Who else could it be—

Just then Scarlett walks past the door, dropping something. With her back to me, she bends down to pick it up. Long blonde hair flows down her back.

Just like in the fucking picture.

Charla's words come back to me, *maybe it was a stripper in the photo.* It hits hard, like a fucking semi plowing into me. Gripping the envelope tighter, I stick it in the drawer. I want to be able to open it in private.

"Scarlett, could you come in here," I state as calmly as my voice will allow. Deep down I'm seething. I can't let her or, shit, Marc see it.

"Marc, you can go." I dismiss him without responding to his concerns. He sighs and shakes his head as he goes, shutting the door behind him.

It leaves Scarlett Ward and me alone.

"How are you?"

"I'm... I'm good," she states, coming to stand by the chair in front of my desk, not sitting.

"That's good. Have you been staying away from Corey?"

"Yes, sir."

"Did he ever send payment?"

Scarlett casts her eyes down and I already know what her answer will be before she even speaks.

"No, he did not."

What a fucking dick. Seriously a desperate dick.

"I see."

I watch Scarlett, studying her. The way she looks back up at me and brushes her hair back. It's almost familiar and I wonder if it's because she's been employed here so long or if it's because of something else.

A thought pops into my mind and I pull out my phone. Pulling up the photo that I had screenshot from the article that was published I place it down on my desk and push it toward Scarlett.

"Do you know this woman?"

Kelly's face is visible. There is no mistaking it.

Scarlett picks up my phone and stares for a few seconds before her eyes look up to mine.

"This is my new neighbor, Kelly Ann, she just moved here."

I slump back in my chair. You've got to be fucking me. I want to bet that Stefan and Corey had a hand in that living arrangement. Scarlett lives in a run-down portion of the city, smack in the center between The Red Society and the beach where Charla resides or resided.

"Why do you have a photo of the two of us, you're not having me watched are you? I told you I would stay away from that man." Her tone is almost nervous, angry maybe.

"Of course not. Where did this woman say she moved from?"

She thinks for a moment. "Um, I'm not sure she ever told me. Why? Is everything okay? Am I being watched?"

"That woman is my mother. She was just released from prison. That photo was published in the local paper." I decide to be honest just to see the reaction it'll pull from her.

Scarlett's hands fly to her face, covering her mouth in shock. "What do you mean she was just released from prison?"

I smile. "I was hoping you would ask. She abused me for many years. My grandfather rescued me from her hands. Surely you must remember this or perhaps your mother might have mentioned it. Have you not seen the news? The girls must be gossiping in the dressing room." They have. I've heard it. Now to see what Scarlett says.

"No." She shakes her head. "I'm sorry, I don't pay attention to those types of things. I have one focus and that's not losing my apartment."

I figured she wouldn't have a clue. She may have started here as a teenager, but I seriously doubt she retained any gossip. Her life has always been moving in survival mode. Like mine once was.

"It seems we have something in common, we were dealt a shit hand as far as having a mother is concerned."

Scarlett stays silent, nodding. I wouldn't be shocked if her own mother didn't abuse her in her younger years. As soon as she was old enough, her mother threw her into stripping. Such a piece of shit thing to do to supply an alcohol addiction.

"You may go, but I'm going to suggest you stay far away

from that woman. Especially if you want to continue here. Is that clear?"

"Yes, sir." She turns and makes her way to the door, stopping just as she gets to it with her hand on the knob. She turns back to look at me. "Sir, I just want you to know, that we only went to lunch that one time. I thought it would be nice to make a new friend. I haven't seen her since. Not once."

"Keep it that way, Scarlett."

I would bet all the cash in my club that their lunch was set up. An opportunity for a photo and then that sick woman went into hiding, probably holed up in that shit hole of a duplex. I feel bad for Scarlett. She could leave and I know she would make it on her own. However, she feels like she owes her mother something, what that is I don't know. That's a story to dig another day.

Once I'm certain she has left and is no longer standing outside my door, I stand and go to lock it. I don't want to be interrupted when I unseal the envelope that is currently burning a hole in my desk drawer.

Pulling it out, I slowly break the seal and slide the papers out. My eyes move fast looking for the words that I am hoping to see in black ink.

And sure enough, halfway down the page, the words are there.

Revenge will be mine.

36

CHARLA

I've lost count of how many nights I've stayed with Spencer. It hasn't been miserable, yet it has. I have a room with a view of the ocean. While it comforts me, I miss the darkness. I miss the trees. I miss him. I know I shouldn't. Maybe he is right and that he is all wrong for a girl like me. It still doesn't change how these feelings I've developed. What I do know is, that I won't allow myself to be treated like less than I deserve.

So why do I scroll social media every so often just to see if I can catch a glimpse of him? I don't know, maybe the reporters will snap a photo of him with some new arm candy. Why am I torturing myself?

Leaving my phone behind, I decide to head outside. The warm sand beneath my toes is almost soothing. The salty air is refreshing. It's exactly what I need to clear my head. I pop down on the sand. Close enough to let the water crash over my toes, but far enough back that my ass won't get wet.

Closing my eyes, I allow the sounds of the ocean to calm all the crazy that I've been feeling. I don't let myself think of the bad boy, my father, or Corey. I picture playing in the waves without a care in the world. My hair matted with sand.

Growing up, I was never allowed to swim in the Atlantic. I mean I could get my feet wet and wade, but that was the extent. Anything more was considered reckless and my father wouldn't have it. I grew up and still have never swam in the salty water. How sad considering I love being on the beach.

Standing, I take a step into the water. It's cold, yet I don't care. Each daring step takes me further. I'm fully clothed. Denim shorts and a light pink crop top.

Before I know it, I'm up to my waist and my shirt now mostly see-through. I still don't care. I bob around, leaning my head back so my hair gets wet. I can't believe I've never done this before. In this moment I feel free. I feel in control of my life. Swimming under, I let the waves bring me to shore before I swim back out and do it again.

Riding a wave to the shore, I stand ready to swim back out again when I catch a figure walking down. My hopeful heart hopes for East but the closer the person walks, the more I realize that it one hundred percent is not him.

Spencer walks up, a strange expression on his face.

"Hey." I give a wave ready to go back out, but his words stop me.

"This is new. Since when do you swim in the ocean?"

See, even he knows I've never played in the ocean before. How sheltered was I? Never mind, not going there.

"I don't know, something came over me and I decided to go out. Want to join me?"

"Definitely not. Besides, you need to come back up to the condo, someone is waiting for you, and um, yeah, your shirt..." My friend trails off, diverting his eyes.

I glance down, well, shit. I didn't think this through. My shirt exposes my pink lace bra that hides nothing. This isn't awkward at all. Wait, though, did he say someone was inside for me?

"Did you say someone was waiting for me?"

Without looking at me, Spencer nods.

"Who? Because if it's my father I'm not up for seeing him."

"It's not your father, now come on. You can have my shirt." He lifts his shirt over his head and holds a hand out. His eyes find mine and I think for the first time ever, he is nervous to see me like this. My eyes skim his tan skin. Smooth ripples form from his chest, all the way down, dipping below his pants. I shouldn't be checking out my best friend. Something is wrong with me.

Walking out of the water, I wring my shirt out, trying to remove as much excess water as I can. I'm curious to know who is waiting for me.

"Jesus, Char, next time wear a swimsuit or something." Spencer grunts as he turns away from me, still holding his shirt. I take it and he quickly walks back in the direction he came.

I laugh. "What's wrong, Spence, do I make you nervous?"

He stops and turns to me, getting directly in my face.

"Does this look like I'm nervous?" He grabs the bulge in his jeans.

I can't help but gasp and take a step back. That I was so not expecting.

"Now come on before something stupid happens."

I stay rooted in place to give us distance. I need distance between us. I cannot have my best friend turned on by the sight of me. I mean yeah, my nipples are exposed through my clothing. And me checking him out, no, just no. He's my best friend. There's no way.

Once I finally start moving, guilt hits me. I shouldn't have been swimming in my clothes. Not like that. It wasn't fair to Spencer. I need to apologize.

Running to catch up, he's already inside and the elevator door is closing with him in it.

Dammit.

I jump in the next one, slamming the button to the top floor, willing the damn thing to go as fast as it can. I want to talk to Spencer before having to deal with whoever is waiting. They can wait. My best friend cannot.

The second the doors open, I push through them. Spencer is rounding the corner.

"Spence, wait!"

He stops as I run to catch up to him. The look on his face is strained and I feel so horrible.

"I'm... I'm sorry. I wasn't thinking clearly. I shouldn't have teased you." The words rush out. I can't seem to help it. I can't lose him.

Sighing, he cups my cheek. At first, it makes me nervous because he's never touched me like this. Like he wants to kiss me. "I'm sorry too, it's just I wasn't expecting to be—" Spencer swallows before going to speak again but is suddenly pulled away from me in one swift motion.

"Do not touch her." That deep voice spits out nothing but anger. I'm in such shock that I don't even know how to process what is happening.

There stands a very angry East.

"She's my best friend. What the fuck are you to her?" Spencer gets right in his face. For a split second I'm worried East will hit him. His fists are balled at his side. The tic in his jaw tells me he is holding back.

"She's mine."

Holy shit! What did East just say? Did I hear him right?

"Is that so? Last I checked, you treated her like shit and who took her in? That would be me. So back off, Sinclair."

"Why were your hands on her and where the hell is your shirt?"

"That's none of your damn business."

The two of them are practically head to head, talking about me as if I'm not standing right here. I should put a stop to it.

"I wonder what Lettie would say about this."

Lettie?

Spencer goes stiff. "Her name is Scarlett. She's more than just a stripper. She has a name." Spencer has gone defensive at the mention of this woman. He stalks away and into his condo, slamming the door behind him. I need to remind myself to ask him about it later. Clearly, it's a touchy subject.

East eyes me up and down. I'm still very wet and still wearing Spencer's shirt that stops just above my knees. Something he just notices. His eyes flare as he processes that Spencer was shirtless and me being the one wearing it.

"Why do you have on his shirt?"

"Uh, I was swimming, and my shirt was a little see-through." I shrug, trying not to make a big deal out of this. Things are already heated.

"Take it off."

"What is it with you and your demands?" I walk past him and hold the door open. He steps inside and then follows me to the room I am staying in. I say nothing as I grab a new bra, panties, and a sundress. When I walk to the bathroom, East follows. He steps into my personal space as I go to shut the door.

"What the hell, East? I need to change."

He pushes through and shuts the door. "So, change."

Ugh! He is so confusing, so frustrating.

I tear Spencer's shirt up over my head and hear East suck in a breath.

"Fuck, Charla."

I won't lie and say his words don't affect me because they do.

37

CHARLA

The space between us is thick. Too thick. I turn away. I begin to remove the rest of my clothing that is sticking to my salty skin. I'm completely naked when East gently tugs on my arm, spinning me back to him.

"Don't ever be afraid to let me see you, to let me see your body."

Hot damn. If he keeps up this kind of talk, I'll be putty in his strong hands before long.

I can't though. He was wrong and until he owns it, I can't be weak. Holding my head high, I pull my arm free, "I'm not. I just didn't think you were worthy of seeing me."

Good job, Charla. I give myself a silent pat on the back. I'm pretty sticky from the salt water. I need to shower, but East is still here, crowding my personal space.

Fuck it. I'm showering. He can say whatever it is he needs to while I'm washing myself.

Walking around him, I lean over and turn the handle to warm. What I really need is a cold shower thanks to the bad boy standing too close. I feel his eyes on my ass. The low growl that leaves his mouth confirms it. I can't help but smile, I still enjoy getting him riled up.

I don't look back as I remove the rest of my clothing and step into the shower. I pull the curtain closed.

East doesn't move and I'm not sure if that should relieve me or not.

"So why are you here, East?"

"I came to see you." He says it so matter of factly like it's normal for him to just show up.

"That's not good enough, try again."

"I came to apologize, and I'd rather do it back at my place."

East apologize? That's probably a first. I finish rinsing off and grab a towel off the rack.

I'm sure to wrap myself up before stepping out. If I'm going to hear the devil himself out, I need to get my head above water. Lord knows the minute the man touches me I may very well drown and all will be forgiven. Especially if he uses his tongue.

"Are you planning on staying in here while I dress?"

"Yes, I've seen all of you. There's no need for me to leave."

Fuck. Why is he like this?

I attempt to keep the towel around me as I slide black lace up my legs. It's a poor attempt and when the towel falls open, I go to catch it, but strong hands beat me to it.

East grips the towel and pulls it away from my body. "I don't know why you are hiding your body from me. You have no reason to hide your perfect body."

I hurry and finish dressing before responding to his words. "You lost the right to get to see me like this when you called me a trust fund baby. I'm not some skank that you just get to look at whenever you want."

East steps in close. So close I can smell the mint on his breath mixed with his cologne. He smells so good it nearly has me squeezing my thighs together. I hate that my body reacts to him. Hate it.

That's a lie.

I love it. Crave it. Even if it is toxic.

When I look up into his eyes, they are angry again.

"You are not some skank. I've never looked at you like you were. I may have said some unkind things, but skank was never one. I'm appalled that you think that's what I view you as. Now let's go so we can talk in private."

I didn't think he had it in him. East is usually so cold and dark. He doesn't do kind.

The anger in his eyes starts to dim as I step closer. "Fine, let's go. I want to hear what you have to say."

East holds the door and gestures for me to step through. The minute I'm past him, he steps up behind me grabbing my hips to still me. "You will forgive me, Charla." He bites my neck once before letting me go so he can walk past me. He glances back smirking.

Asshole.

He knows what he's doing. Hell, even I know what he is doing. What's more, I let him do it. His mouth on me is one thing I crave the most.

On our way out, I stop by Spencer's room to let him know I am leaving with East for a bit. I made East wait in the foyer, he was less than thrilled but I stood my ground. Speaking to my best friend alone is something I had to do. Spencer, himself, wasn't too thrilled with me agreeing to go with the devil. These two are going to be the death of me. That is, of course, if my father doesn't beat them to it.

Once in East's slick black car, it dawns on me, no Burns. "Why isn't Burns driving you?"

He gives me a quick glance. "You want to know the truth?"

"Yes."

"He wouldn't shut up about you, so I sent him on vacation."

Oh my. I'm curious to know what Burns was saying but I'm not about to ask. I have enough on my mind and don't need some old man's thoughts added to the mix.

For the next fifteen minutes, we drive in silence. For that, I'm glad. I need time to think. Will I forgive East? Should I?

I'm so lost in my own head that I didn't even realize that we've turned around. East is on the phone, a hard expression across his face.

Without thinking, I reach over and squeeze his thigh. He instantly tenses, giving me a sideways glance. Immediately, I feel guilty. He doesn't like to be touched. My face heats as I quickly remove my hand and turn to look back out the window. I don't want him to see my embarrassment.

"We have to stop by The Red Society. Something has come up."

Great, just the place I want to go. "Okay," I reply quietly.

"It should not take long."

Again, I reply with okay. What else is there to say? It's not like I had any plans today or tonight for that matter. I'm just along for the ride at this point until we sit down and talk.

East pulls into the parking lot, I expect to just stay in his car. After all, he said it won't take long. So when he rounds the car and opens my door, I give him a puzzled look.

"What are you doing? Get out of the car."

"I figured I would just wait here." Plus, I really don't

want to go in there. Too many memories of past shit shows haunt me. I won't tell him that though.

"You absolutely will not be waiting in the car. Now get out."

Rolling my eyes, I slowly get out just to make a statement. It annoys him and knowing it does, brings me great pleasure.

His deep voice comes up behind me as I walk. "I'm sure the last thing you want or need is someone snapping a photo of you alone in a car, looking like a stalker or better yet, desperate."

He's right. Again. I hate it when he is right, but photographers and reports don't care. They will spin anything in a way that brings in money.

We walk in the front doors and instantly it's like I traveled back in time. Sitting with Spencer in a lounge. Rushing up the stairs to confront East, only to find some stripper on her knees. Shaking the dark memories, I look around. While it's only six pm, the lights are already low. The red glow illuminates the entire place. There are quite a bit of men here already. Don't they have other things to do on a Saturday night?

"Marc will show you to my office. You are to wait in there for me."

I nod, not bothering to fight him on his stupid demands. A tall, husky man walks up to us as East winks once. "I'm sure you remember my office."

His parting words set my face on fire along with something else. Jealously? No, I have no right to be jealous, yet it creeps up as I picture him walking up to me with his cock out, glistening with the stripper's spit.

I'm thankful for the red glow right now. Otherwise,

Marc would see how red I am, and I know he'd get a kick out of it.

After following East's security guy up a flight of stairs, he leads me to the office. He opens the door and steps aside. As soon as I enter, he shuts it, leaving me there alone. *Well, isn't he friendly?*

Glancing around his office, I check everything out. His bookcases hold framed articles, a few praising East for being one of the county's wealthiest men.

Last year to be exact.

Holy shit.

I read it two more times. I wasn't expecting that. I mean, I knew, well, assumed East did well financially based on his clothes, house, and having a personal driver. But shit.

I debate on snooping through his desk, but as my hand reaches the drawer, I stop, deciding against it. I don't want to know what he keeps in there. Instead, I hop on his desk and wait for him.

38

EAST

The cameras caught Corey snooping around back. Probably looking for Scarlett. Little does he know, Marc has been driving her to and from work since she told me about my mother being her neighbor. I trust no one and I know Corey and Stefan are behind this bullshit.

After looking over the cameras a second time and seeing him get into a car, and drive off, we can only assume he left. I leave Marc to let the other members know to be on high alert. There's a blonde in my office reminding me I have something else to handle.

I rush up the stairs in a haste. The need to be near Charla is strong. Why that is, I don't know. The one thing I know is that I need to apologize and have her body one last time before her world as she knows it, is turned upside down.

When that happens, she'll hate me.

I don't bother knocking, it's my office after all.

The sight in front of me when I open the door is one I'm not expecting. However, my dick responds, twitching.

There on my desk sits the most beautiful blonde I've

ever had in my office and believe me, there's been plenty over the years. No one compares to her though. No one.

Charla's yellow dress rests just above her thighs, legs slightly parted. Just seeing her like this makes me want to take her right here and now. Even the bulge in my pants is begging to be set free.

Maybe I'll worry about apologizing later.

I swallow thickly, hoping to regain some sort of control. It's useless though because she flashes me a devilish grin. It's as if she knows what she is doing to me. Closing my door quickly, I reach Charla in three long strides.

I force her legs apart and come to stand between them.

"That's not how you apologize." She makes a poor attempt to push me back to try to close her legs. Too bad, I'm stronger, faster. My hand reaches between her legs. She stops fighting instantly. Ever so slightly, I run my fingers on the outside of the thin fabric. It's wet.

She's always wet for me.

My dick strains harder, reminding me that he wants to come out to play.

"East," she half whimpers, letting me know she wants to fight me but also that she wants this. She should fight me. We are a fucked up mix.

"I have full intentions of giving you a proper explanation for my behavior and I will, but." I slide one finger under the band and push inside her pussy.

Soaked.

"Right now I need to taste you."

Small pants leave her mouth, her eyes are filled with desire. Once I'm certain she won't resist or lose her shit on me, I remove my finger, taking her panties with me. She allows me to slide them down her legs, tossing them to the floor.

Pulling her ass closer to the edge of my desk, I drop down. There in front of me is her pretty, pink pussy. Glistening, waiting to be touched. I breathe in the drug that is her scent before swiping my tongue across her slit once.

Charla's head falls back. That won't do. I want her to watch. "I want you to watch me. Watch what I do to your body. Understand?"

Her green eyes look down at me as if I'm torturing her.

Keeping my eyes on hers, my tongue darts out again and again. She writhes at my touch. She fights hard to keep her eyes on me. The moment I suck on her swollen clit, her hands fist my hair, pulling me closer to her. As if I'm too far away.

That's my girl.

I insert a finger while continuing to assault her with my tongue. She's close, I can tell by how she reacts to me. Her moans grow louder.

The door opens suddenly behind me, causing Charla to freeze.

"Oh my god, Corey! What the hell are you doing here?" She makes to push me away and I let her, but I don't allow her to close her legs. Oh no. He's brought to me at the perfect time. I stand up and step aside, keeping a hand on her thigh, gripping it hard. I want him to see Charla. I want him to see how I satisfy her. Let him see her pussy juices on my face.

"What a pleasant surprise."

"Fuck off. I'm calling the police, holding me here like this."

I laugh a sinister laugh. "Call them. You have a no trespassing order. Technically." I pull a pocketknife and not some cheap one, from my back pocket. "I could kill you right now and get away with it. You trespassed, harassing my employees. You shouldn't be here, and I won't hesitate to end you."

Corey's eyes go wide as the color drains from his face. Good.

"East," Charla begs. I want to tell her to relax and that I won't really kill him. I just want to scare the fucker.

"Marc, sit him in a chair, I think it's time he gets a lesson on how to pleasure a woman."

"Um, East..." Charla's voice cracks. She's nervous. Even better.

I spread Charla's legs a little further. "Charla's pussy tastes divine, it's a shame you never enjoyed it."

Corey's eyes are on her. He glares, unable to look away. I spread her lips apart allowing him to see how wet she is.

"A real man does this. See how wet she is for me, for my mouth to be on her." I insert a finger, causing a quiet moan to escape her lips. Removing my finger, I bring it to my lips, sucking her sweet juices right off my finger.

Corey watches my every move. He's mad as fuck. He should be. He just lost the best thing he never had.

"A real man gives his woman what she wants. He doesn't violate her. You seem to have a problem with that."

"Fuck you," he spits out. I shake my head. Assholes like him will never learn. However, I plan to devour Charla's cunt right in front of him. Let him know what he's missing.

Marc clears his throat. Shit. Marc. I forgot he was here. The thought of him seeing my girl exposed sends rage throughout my bones. No one should be able to see Charla like this except me. I clamp my anger down though. I can't be losing my shit when I'm the one who has a blonde perched on my desk with her juices spilling out all over it while taunting her pathetic excuse of an ex.

Fuck it. I'll use this moment to claim her. Let both see

who she belongs to. Dropping back to my knees, I thrust two fingers deep inside of Charla. She cries out. Pleasure oozes from her lips.

"Hear that? She loves what I do to her. Don't you, baby?"

Charla moans in response.

Such a good girl.

I swipe my tongue back up her slit. She nearly arches off the table. I can't help but smirk while sucking on her sweet cunt. She's wound so tight that it only takes minutes to bring her to orgasm. She cries out my name while fisting my hair. Pride flows through my veins as I claim her.

Without any shame, I stand back up and move to the side.

"You see this?" I point my finger at Charla's swollen, dripping pussy. "This is how you take care of a woman. This is how you please her."

Corey's face is red, veins popping. Anger evident. Marc on the other hand looks a little uncomfortable, yet I'm sure he likes what he saw. He's watched and even joined in a time or two in the past. I've never minded sharing before. Charla, however, is off limits. I will never share her. That rage is back. Red hot rage that suddenly makes me possessive is something I've never experienced.

Very quickly, I pull her dress to cover her. They've seen enough. I pull Charla up slowly. Her breathing is still somewhat heavy and the urge to bring her home is strong. Stronger than I thought possible. I lean in, biting her neck before sucking on it. Just like that, her hands are back in my hair. It takes damn near all my control to pull back when all I want to do is bend her over my desk and fuck her until she collapses.

As much as I want that, I still need to get shit squared away here.

"You are never to touch her. Understand?" I practically growl the words at my security guard.

"Yes, sir," Marc replies straight away.

"East," Charla whispers, bringing my attention back to her. "I want to go now."

The way she says it isn't that she wants to leave because she is upset. No, it is quite the opposite. She wants to go so that I can fuck her brains out.

"We'll go."

Standing, I walk up real close to Corey. I shove my fingers under his nose. "Her scent is delicious, like a drug one can't get enough of. It must suck to know you'll never taste her again."

Yup, I'm that asshole.

"Marc, call the police, have Corey arrested for trespassing."

Without another word, I take Charla's hand in mine, leading her out of the room.

39

CHARLA

The drive back to East's place is quiet. It gives me time to replay what happened back in his office. Two men watched as East fucked me with his mouth. I should be ashamed. I should feel humiliated. I feel anything but. Instead, I found it thrilling, erotic, knowing that other eyes were on us. I'm starting to think something might truly be wrong with me. Or maybe I'm just finding myself and no longer caring what anyone else thinks. The truth is, the security dude could have filmed the entire thing and I wouldn't have cared at all. When East touches me, everything else falls away. I'm floating and free.

Then there are the statements he has made. No one is to ever touch me. Did he claim me back in that office? What did he mean? It doesn't make sense. East has stated many times that he doesn't do relationships. He doesn't do sweet. He's all wrong for me. His possessive actions back in the office send my mind into a tailspin.

Arriving back at East's place, he quietly leads me up the stairs to his side. I hesitate a moment until he tugs me to keep going. We walk into a dark room. I remember this room. It was the first room I walked into, and the light switch didn't work. I stay still by the door, waiting for East's next move. Within seconds the room is lit up in an orange glow. He stands next to a side table with an old lamp. At least it looks old. He doesn't smile. His expression is unreadable.

I watch in silence as he walks over to a fireplace. He takes a match off the mantle and lights it, tossing the stick into the fireplace. East repeats the process and slowly flames come to life, dancing among the logs that have blackened by past burnings.

When my eyes meet East's, all the air seems to leave the room. Fire flickers in his eyes. Orange flames reflect off of his lip ring. It's haunting, to see him in this light. There's a tic in his jaw. He looks like he is fighting an inner battle and I'm not sure I want to be in the crossfire when he finally explodes. Been there, done that.

Keeping my eyes on him, he stalks over to the opposite side of the room and reaches down. It's then that I notice the stacks of newspapers. Stacks upon stacks line the room. He holds one up, reading a line.

"Mother admits abusing her son out of pure enjoyment."

The hate in his tone is so clear that it causes me to flinch.

"What will be worse, a boy living with an abusive mom or living among strippers and sex?"

East doesn't stop. He reads line after line. His traumatic

childhood blasted for everyone to read. Tears quietly fall down my face.

> *"Sinclair pulled from public school over taunts. But could it be so he could spend more time looking at naked women?"*

My heart breaks all over for the broken devil in front of me. I watch in silence, unable to form words as he walks back to the fire and tosses the newspaper in.

"They have no idea how tormented I was. How these stories made my life and my grandfather's life a living hell. It was almost as bad as the abuse I suffered."

His confession guts me.

"My grandfather pulled me from the public school system after the bullying didn't stop. It was vicious. Who attacks the victim?"

I walk up close wanting to comfort him. I pause, not really knowing if that is what he wants. I picture a cold, heartless man who doesn't want to be touched.

He stares at me. "I'm sorry for the cruel words I said to you. You've lived in this perfect bubble of a life, Charla. How does it feel seeing our picture all over social media? How did it feel seeing all the comments, the speculations, knowing not a single person had any idea of the truth, the facts?"

Tears fall harder now, I can only shake my head. Doesn't matter how it made me feel. People talk, they make up whatever they want. They don't care who they hurt in the process.

East tosses another paper into the flames. He watches it burn as if the ink disappearing and turning to ash somehow erases the damage that's been done.

"I was a child, a victim, that got bullied instead of receiving support from our community. Of course, my grandfather paid for years of counseling, but what was the point? I learned to trust no one. I shut down, went cold, and the man standing in front of you is what you get." East flashes me a sinister smile. One that causes goosebumps to form on my skin.

Now more than ever, I have a glimpse into the inner mind of East Sinclair. I know why he is so cold. Why he hates and doesn't do intimacy. It makes me sad for him. His confession alone tells me that East isn't all bad. Deep down buried is a man who once was a boy who was done wrong.

"Why all the newspapers?" I ask.

"My grandfather would pack me up in the early hours of the morning and drive all around town to the newspaper stands. He would put the coins in and if our names were mentioned, he'd take every last paper. He tried damn hard to prevent people from gossiping about us. He really did. In the end, though, it did not matter. People still received newspapers, they gossiped anyway."

"I give your grandfather a lot of credit for doing that. He was trying to protect you."

After letting the fire die out, East walks me back to the room I briefly stayed in. He doesn't come in, staying in the doorway.

"Charla, I want you to know that I'm sorry for accusing you of having a part in the bullshit that your father has brought to the surface. That woman being released because of your father has opened up a lot of locked-up memories. I won't sugar coat. I fucking hate your father. He belongs in hell for the games he plays."

I cringe at his hateful words. They hurt, even still, his

feelings are valid, and I will not downplay or make excuses for my father's doing.

"You deserve to feel the way you do, East."

He nods once and starts to retreat. Just the thought of him going back to his room alone doesn't sit well with me. It's why I go after him.

40

EAST

"Stay with me."

Those three words. They do something to my heart. Shaking my head, I try to put more space between us.

"I need to call the club to make sure everything was handled properly with Corey."

"So, call. I'm not going anywhere, East."

I keep quiet because the need to take Charla is still in the front of my mind. I still want to bend her over and fuck her into oblivion. What I don't want is the pity. I don't want nor do I need pity.

Charla follows me into my room as I dial Marc's cell. Leaning up against my dresser, I undo the top buttons of my shirt. He answers on the second ring.

"Status update."

As Marc starts to fill me in, Charla comes to stand in front of me. She studies me before licking her lips and dropping to her knees. Hands come up to unbutton and unzip my slacks. Can this woman get any sexier? She looks up at me through dark lashes, flashing me a wink. My dick hardens in anticipation of what's to come. Her pink lips part as her tongue darts out, licking me from my base to my head.

Low curses leave my mouth as I bite the silver ring in my lip. It causes Marc to ask if everything is all right.

"Yes, I'll check in later." I hang up without waiting for him to respond.

After tossing my cell on the dresser, my hands grip her silky blonde hair. Her lips finally envelop me while keeping her eyes on me. I swear it's like her mouth was made for my dick and my dick alone.

Charla's free hand finds my balls as she teases and sucks. I grip her hair, forcing her to take me deeper. Tears well in the corner of her eyes from me hitting the back of her throat, yet she doesn't stop. She fucking takes me. Takes all of me. She takes it when I'm rough and hard. Even when I'm hateful. This woman is still here, sucking my dick right now like her life depends on it.

Again, something constricts in my chest. I'm not sure I like it. It makes me feel things, too many things, so I pull out roughly and pull Charla up by her hair. Her cries only make my dick throb. I fucking love the sounds that leave her mouth.

I let go of her hair only to grab her wrist and drag her over to my bed. In one swift move, I rip her dress down and off of her. Her panties were left behind at the office and they better be exactly where I left them when I yanked them off. Charla is a fucking sight. Perfect tits. Curves and a bare pussy. She's perfect. I turn her around and push her face down on my bed before dragging her ass to the edge. I slap it once, causing her to yelp. I then remove my clothes faster than I think I ever have.

With her ass up, I spread her and drive my dick straight

into her waiting pussy. Charla gasps. She wasn't expecting me to drive in so hard and so fast without foreplay. Hell, I didn't either, but spreading her cheeks apart and seeing her perfect cunt ignited a fire and I had to take her.

It's been days since I've had her last and knowing this is probably the last time I'll ever fuck her has me thrusting into her hard. Her moans are like music to my ears, especially as she comes undone underneath me. I enjoy knowing only I can bring her this kind of pleasure.

Reaching forward, I grab the back of her hair, pulling her to me. Gripping her chin, I force her to turn my way. Something inside of me takes over and my lips crash into hers hard. I need to taste her. I want her to feel what I feel when we are both like this. Her tongue tangles with mine. Like a good girl, she takes what I dish out and even tries to match me. God, I'm going to miss her.

I'm insatiable still as I pull away and push her back down. Grabbing her hip, I pull her further back to the point I am holding the lower half of her body. Gripping her hard, I continue to slam into her. I spit on her ass and take my free hand to rub my spit down her crack. She tenses a little but the minute I take my finger and push through the tight barrier, she screams out my name. For some reason, she's perfectly fine with what I'm doing to her. I don't know why that is. The fact that she trusts me with her body makes my heart quicken. This time when she comes apart while grasping at the black sheets, I do the same. Spilling into her cunt one last time as my hold on her hips doesn't lessen. There will be bruises.

I pull out and flip her over. I'm not finished with her yet. She's still coming down from her high. Her eyes flutter as I slide her spent body to the center of the bed. I hover above her and enter slowly.

"No more, East. I can't." She whimpers softly.

"Yes, you can. I'll be gentle."

"You don't do gentle. You are hard and dark. I don't think you know the meaning of gentle."

Her legs relax, allowing me to go deeper. I continue moving slowly just to prove to her that I can do gentle. For her, I can. I want her to know I can. To feel that I can be gentle.

Why I want her to know this, I'm not entirely sure. She has my mind all fucked up with feelings and other shit that will not matter in a couple of hours.

After tomorrow, all secrets will be exposed. She will hate me. I one hundred percent can guarantee she will hate me.

Because I will be the one exposing the lie she has lived her entire life.

41

CHARLA

I wake up alone. In East's bed. He left a note on the pillow saying that he had business to take care of and that Burns would be waiting for me when I was ready.

I won't lie, it stings a little to wake up alone without him, especially after last night. First, he fucked me thoroughly, then he made love to me. I know he doesn't love me, but East Sinclair made love to me. He worshipped my body and was so gentle. That man has never been gentle ever.

I decide to skip a shower. I can take one as soon as I get to Spencer's. My dress still lays on the floor. I pick it up, the neckline is stretched out. Oh well, it'll have to do. I don't have any other clothes here.

Once I make my way downstairs, I spot Burns sitting by the front window. "Good morning."

He turns in my direction and smiles. "It's good afternoon now. Nearly one pm." His eyes go wide as they land on my neck.

Oh my god!

The old man stands. "Are you ready to go?"

I nod, feeling too foolish to reply. Between the time and just thinking of what my neck must look like, I just want to go home.

The drive home is quiet as I stare out the window. My phone must have died overnight and never placed on charge. Personally, I don't care. I don't want to deal with real life right now. Last night is all I can focus on. Something shifted between us. I felt it. I know he did too. I could see it in his eyes. Every single time he stared into mine, I felt it. Like this could be something more. The thought is ludicrous. Even still. I know there was something more and when his mouth claimed mine, it was more than pent-up anger and hate. Dare I say it was passionate?

Telling Burns thank you, I climb out and realize there are reporters everywhere. Cameras and all. How did I not notice them when we pulled up?

What the hell?

"There she is!" someone yells, and they all turn to look at me. Hell. I look like shit. Hickeys on my neck. My dress is wrinkled and stretched out, my hair is in a messy bun and I'm carrying my heels in my hand. Panic rises. Everything becomes a blur as I move fast through the lobby as I hear them calling after me. Some scream my name. Some cameras flash as they snap my picture. I try not to pay any attention, the goal is to get on the elevator as quickly as possible. Once in, I pound the floor number hard.

What catches my attention as the doors close is the one reporter. The one with shaggy brown hair that asks me what I think of my father having a mystery child.

The entire way I curse myself for letting my phone die. In a time like this, my phone actually being charged could come in handy. I love the silence and being detached, but right now I need my phone more than ever.

The elevator doors open and I'm grateful to find no paparazzi on our floor. I run straight down to Spencer's door and punch in the key code. I enter quickly, shutting and locking the door behind me. It's quiet, I don't hear any noise, so I doubt my best friend is home. I rush into my bedroom and plug my phone in. Giving it a few minutes to charge, I go into the bathroom to brush my teeth and wash my face.

When I return to my cell that's sitting on my night-stand, I power it on.

My phone goes insane with text alerts. With each new alert, my heart sinks. The words the guy spoke as the elevator doors shut repeat over and over.

Twenty alerts.

That's not a good sign. I take a deep breath opening the first one. It's from East.

> Sorry

Such a vague text.

I open the next one, this one, from my father.

> Charla, we need to talk.
> Charla, I said we need to talk.
> You need to stop being defiant and answer.
> Answer me.
> It's not what you think. Call me so I can explain.

A new type of dread fills me with each text message I read. So much dread that I can't keep reading his. I hit the back button I see that Spencer sent me a few as well.

Where the hell are you?
Do you need me to come get you?
Dammit your phone is going straight to voicemail
Are you okay?
Please respond. I'm worried.
Do you think it's true?
Don't come through the front doors.
Reporters are everywhere.

Ha. I can only laugh at the irony in that last text. If only my phone was on to let me know what I was walking into. However, the one asking if I think it is true makes me nauseous. Is Spencer referring to what the pap said to me?

My phone rings, startling me. Spencer's name flashes across the screen.

"Hey."

"Oh my god, where have you been?! Never mind, are you safe?" Spencer's frantic words worry me. Something is seriously wrong. I feel it in my gut.

"I'm at your place. My phone died while with East last night."

"Thank god! Stay there! Don't leave. I'm on my way."

I hear a woman's voice in the background. She asks him if that's a good idea. I want to question yet don't. Spencer mumbles to her before hanging up without so much as a goodbye.

That was strange.

But not as strange as what seems to be unfolding right in front of me.

I manage to find the courage to open social media to click on one of the local news stations.

The headlines that appear one after another make me wish I hadn't.

STEFAN KRAUSS HAS ANOTHER DAUGHTER!

STEFAN KRAUSS, THE MAYOR HAS A MYSTERY DAUGHTER. BUT WAIT THERE'S MORE!

CHARLA'S TWIN SISTER IS FOUND!

The last headline has me dropping my phone and running to the bathroom to spill the contents in my stomach.

42

CHARLA

I feel someone lifting me off the floor in the bathroom. I don't bother to open my eyes to find out who it is. What's the point?

After vomiting, I called my father. He began to ramble, and I had to scream into the phone to get his attention.

"I'll have this silenced soon. Just give me some— "

"Father."

"This will die down and it'll be like it never happened."

What? How can someone say such a thing? Especially if it's true that he has another daughter. My father continues to spew words out of his mouth. Words I don't want to even hear because it proves just how heartless he is.

"Father, is it— "

"Just lie low and let me get this handled."

"FATHER!"

"Jesus, Charla, what?"

"Is it true?"

"Don't worry about— "

"Is it true?" I grit my teeth together. I'm pissed, hurt,

disgusted. So many emotions and this man is still trying to brush things under the rug.

My father, Stefan Krauss, sighs, letting me know without a doubt that this is in fact true.

"Yes, but I can explain all of that over dinner."

My heart breaks. I have had a sister this entire time and yet lived as an only child. "Explain now."

"Charla, not now."

"You will tell me now or I'll hang up this phone and never speak to you again."

"Dammit, Charla, fine! I met your birth mom at a strip club. You already know this." *My father sighs again and I sit up against the toilet for fear I may get sick again.*

"She got pregnant and well she was carrying twins, two girls, fraternal."

Closing my eyes, I will my upset stomach to calm down. I'm a twin. I have a fucking twin somewhere.

"I couldn't have that in the papers, my career was on the rise. I had an agreement drawn up. Rochelle signed away."

So, Rochelle is my mother's name. He's never told me. It doesn't surprise me that he would have some sort of paperwork involved. It also proves just what a cold-hearted person he is.

"I... I have a sister, a twin." *Saying the words out loud for the first time in my life causes silent tears to stream down my face.*

"Yes, we agreed that we each got one baby. I paid her a huge sum so that she and her daughter could live a comfortable life." *My father sounds frustrated to be telling me all this, and it only pisses me off further. He has zero right to be annoyed over his actions.*

"Where are they now?"

"I don't know. When I left the hospital with you, they lived in the next town over. I never looked back. No reason. Documents were signed."

"You're an asshole," I say before hanging up the phone and vomiting all over again.

"Shh, it'll be okay."

I'm sobbing into someone's chest as they lift me up. I lean back to see that it is my best friend.

When I hung up on my father, I lost it. First, I was sick, then I was angry, and then I couldn't control the sobs that left my body.

Now everything hurts. And not in a good way. *Not in the way East leaves me hurting.*

"I'm so sorry, Char."

Pulling back, I look him straight in the eyes. "Don't do that. Don't apologize for my father's actions." The last thing I want is people apologizing for him.

"What are you going to do now?"

"I don't know. I mean, I guess I need to look my sister up. I don't know where to start, like I don't even know her name."

Spencer stiffens underneath me and it causes me to pause. Lifting my head from his chest, I ask, "What?"

His green eyes search mine with a worried look across his face. "What if I told you I found her so to speak."

I jerk away from him. "What? How? Did you know?!" I'm frantic and all sorts of emotional at this point.

"Calm down, no, I didn't know. Not until the papers released the article."

"Then how! How do you know my sister, Spence?"

I watch as he nervously runs his fingers through his hair. What the fuck is he about to tell me?

"I'm sort of dating her."

Words fail me. He's dating her?! How is that even possible? I don't want to, wait no I can't hear anymore. I turn, running out of the room, and out of my best friend's place. I run straight to the beach. Where the sand meets the water.

It is then that I truly lose it along with everything that I once knew to be my life.

———

The sun has since gone down, yet I haven't let this spot. I'm wet and cold but can't seem to make myself move. I think I hate my father. Those are strong words that I have never taken lightly. However, I lived my entire life lonely with no siblings. I had nannies, and this entire time I had a twin. I wonder how much we look alike. I have so many questions and no answers.

"Charla." Demanding words sound from behind me. I don't turn to look to see who it is. I already know. The sad thing is, I'm not sure I want to see him right now. Not while my life is in shambles.

So much for the perfect life he thinks I live.

East squats down in front of me. He's dressed in black jeans, a black shirt, and black sneakers. I swear he knows no other color, well, except red maybe.

"You're shivering. You need to come inside."

"I'm fine. You can go," I snap avoiding his eyes. My words make him flinch. I don't mean to, and it's not fair to him that I'm being rude. It's just I have nothing more to give anyone.

"I know you are upset. You have every reason to be. However, if you stay out here, you'll end up coming down with something. Now let me walk you back to Spencer's."

"I just want to be alone."

"I'll leave you alone once I get you inside and run a warm bath."

A warm bath sounds heavenly right about now. Giving in, I nod, standing.

The walk back up to the condo is quiet. East doesn't say a single word as we walk. His hand stays on the small of my back with each step. Even when we step into the elevator, he never removes his hand. It's almost comforting.

Walking through the door, Spencer is sitting on his white couch. He stands immediately. "Char, look, I'm so sorry."

I shake my head. I have zero energy for anything more tonight. Tomorrow is another day and maybe, just maybe, I'll be able to handle more. Tonight, though, I'm mentally drained.

"I'm going to run her a bath." East's words are clipped. Maybe he is still annoyed with Spencer and me from yesterday.

Yesterday. What a difference a day makes. How quickly things change. The illusion of the life I have lived is just that, A perfectly shattered illusion full of broken truths.

East starts the bath before removing my clothes. He's respectful, keeping his eyes on mine the entire time. Those haunting eyes never stray away. It's as if he values me in a sense. After last night maybe he sees me as more than a fuck. Not that it matters because That is just something that I can't deal with right now. My life is a lie and I need to sort it out before I can even think of any sort of relationship.

After carefully helping me step in, East takes a cloth and runs it down my back. It's soothing. The water helps to thaw my cold skin, allowing me to relax slightly.

When East finishes washing me, I lean back against the

tub, closing my eyes. It grows quiet. Maybe he left. After all, he said he would. My heart doesn't allow me to peek.

All too soon, the silence is interrupted when the bathroom door opens.

"Did you tell her?"

Spencer has me sitting up, not bothering to cover the top half of my naked body.

"Tell me what?" I demand, looking between both men.

"Charla, you need to cover yourself." East stands abruptly to block Spencer from seeing me.

"She needs to know." There goes Spencer saying things that make no sense to me. It only irritates me further knowing they are keeping something from me.

"Not right now."

Shoving East back, I say, "You're hiding something from me. Tell me now."

Something passes across his face, fear maybe, or even regret. It passes too quickly for me to process.

"Your twin sister works for me, at The Red Society."

I suck in a breath. My twin is a stripper? Like our mother? This must be some cruel joke.

"Tell her the rest, Sinclair."

There's a tic in East's jaw and he swallows before speaking. "I had DNA collected on you and your sister. She is your fraternal twin."

"And?" I don't even want to know how he gathered our DNA, but that's a story for another day.

"I was the one who sent it into the newspaper. To get back at your father."

Rage fills me. How could he do this to me? How could he? I stand up in the bath not giving a fuck who sees me.

"Get out. Now."

"Charla—" East is still trying to cover my naked body like he's some kind of loyal man. He's not. He's the devil.

"No East, don't you Charla me. GET. OUT. NOW." I shove at him again and he puts his hands up in defeat.

"I'll go. I didn't want to hurt you. That was never my intention, I just wanted your father held accountable."

"Go away, East. You too, Spencer."

Miraculously, they both listen and retreat out of the bathroom, allowing me to be alone once again.

Sinking back down into the water, I shake my head.

What a fucking shit show.

After getting out of the tub, I grab my phone from the bed. I tell myself I won't call East to ask if he was the one who really sent in proof. Deep down I know he did. He said he did. I just don't want to believe it. Before I can stop myself, my phone is already pressed to my ear as I wait for him to pick up.

"Charla," his deep voice answers on the third ring. I hate that my breath catches at the sound of his voice. *Focus, Charla.*

"Is it true?"

There's a long moment of silence, so quiet I pull my phone from my ear to make sure we were not disconnected. The green bar lets me know we are still connected.

"East, answer me, please."

"Yes."

That one word. That one word somehow hurts more than everything else. That one word means he knew this about me and never said a word about it.

Without saying goodbye, I hang up. What more is there to say?

43

CHARLA

I powered off my phone the minute I hung up on East. Staring at it now, I contemplate, wondering if it would be better if I left it off.

It would.

So that's just what I do. I leave it off for the next three days.

44

CHARLA

I've decided I have had enough time to process the bomb of a lie that's been dropped at my feet. I've cried, yelled, cried some more. I was angry, still am. Even so, I will hold my head high and move forward. I'm taking my life back. I will be in control. My father has done enough damage to enough people. No more.

I stare at myself as I finish applying my lipstick. Fire engine red. My hair is curled perfectly. The tight black dress I'm wearing stops right above my knees. It hugs me in all the right places, showing off my curves. My breasts peek out of the low v-neckline. Walking over to the closet, I pull a pair of red Jessica Simpson heels out. My favorite pair.

Powering on my cell, I walk out of the room. It's expected that my phone blows up with notifications and alerts. I clear every last one without a second glance. There's nothing I need to see. Nothing at all.

Making my way to the kitchen, I smell coffee. Good. The condo is quiet while I pour the dark liquid into a travel mug before grabbing cream and sugar. I have things to do and people to see.

When I step into the elevator, my nerves kick up a notch. But only because there could be reporters camped out. Charla is not hiding. I'm walking out those front doors and no camera will stop me. In fact, I hope there is, so they see just who I am.

I smile when I see a few reporters lingering just outside the glass doors. Flashes go off before one speaks to me. "Do you have anything to say about learning you have a twin sister?"

Smiling, I look directly at the camera. "Looks like your favorite mayor is a lie. A cheat. If he can lie about having another child, what else has he lied about? I bet if you do some digging, you'll find dirt on both him and Corey Richards." I wink once before sauntering off.

Daddy can suck on that because his daughter is on a war path.

I make it to Daddy's office in less than twenty minutes. That's a new record. In the past, I would take my sweet time going to his place of work. I loathe going into his building, having to put on a front, a fake smile. Not today though. Nope. As I walk in, my smile is genuine.

"Good morning, Charla, it's been a while since I've seen your beautiful face."

Monica, his secretary, sure knows how to act. Her Botox-injected lips smack together to form a smile. It's as fake as her tits. I am very certain they are fake anyway.

"It is a good morning. Is my father in?"

"He is, but I'm afraid he's in meetings this morning."

"Perfect." I clap my hands together. Show time.

I head off toward Daddy's conference room as Botox lips calls out after me. I ignore her. Nothing she says will have me not following through with what I'm about to do.

Just knowing my father is surrounded by others, who

are probably just as fucked up as him, makes this payback a little sweeter.

I walk right in without knocking. The room falls silent as all eyes land on me. A few linger on my chest, especially Corey's. He looks like a drooling dog as his mouth parts while his eyes undress me. Such a pig.

"Good morning, fellows," I say cheerfully.

"Charla, dear. It's good to see you. Did Monica not tell you I was in a meeting?" It's just like him, all business.

Smiling brightly, I look at my father, the stranger in front of me. "Oh she did, I just didn't care."

Gasps fill the silence and, for some sick reason, it brings pleases me.

"Charla, we will talk at lunch."

"I think we'll talk now. See, you lived a lie and forced me to live one too. I need you to confirm everything you told me on the phone."

"Charla, I said we'll talk— "

"No, we will talk now. You don't call the shots anymore."

"Charla, come on, cut your dad a break."

"Shut it, Corey. A man who puts his hands on a woman against her wishes has no say in this matter."

More gasps.

Oh, how I am enjoying this. Killing two birds with one stone.

Corey sinks back, casting his eyes down. I guess he has nothing more to say.

"Now, Daddy, I need you to verify what you told me."

With his face red, he finally speaks, "You have a twin, your birth mother took her. Your birth mother's name is Rochelle and your sister was named Scarlett. Ward was the last name at the time. At least that is what it was when I paid Rochelle off."

"You paid her off?" someone asks.

He doesn't respond.

I'm glad he looks like the asshole he truly is in front of his colleagues.

"Father, I'll also be going back to my condo. You will sign it over to me, no questions asked."

My father goes to speak, anger evident as veins start to protrude on his forehead. However, I'm faster and cut him off. "This will not be discussed further. See, you slyly filled out that lease to control me, your adult daughter. The daughter you've lied to. You kept my sister, my twin, from me my entire life."

If the room wasn't silent before, it is now. All eyes are on my father.

"Will that be all?"

"As a matter of fact, no. Spencer is to be reimbursed for allowing me to stay with him while you kicked me out because you didn't approve of East. You need to reimburse him too."

My father stands quickly, slamming his palms on the conference table. "If you hadn't gotten involved with that punk, we wouldn't be in this mess."

"Don't give me that, you should have just stayed out of my personal relationships and not pushed Corey, who is straight scum, on me. East is more man than Corey will ever be." I refuse to let my father think he is right.

"I keep control because it is clear, you don't know how to."

"Shut up! I expect a new contract at my door by five pm."

Storming out, I slam the door behind me. Why is my

father such a terrible person? That's a question I have asked myself numerous times over the past seventy-two hours. I'll never get an answer.

Monica stands quickly as I come up. "I hope you didn't interrupt your father, you know how— "

"Fuck off," I reply, not even bothering to engage in conversation. The sound of my heels clicking on the pristine white tile is the only sound I focus on as I leave, rushing, wanting to get the hell out of there.

45

EAST

I knew releasing Stefan's paternity bullshit would cause Charla heartache. I knew she would hate me when she learned it was me who sent the results to the paper.

Even still, I didn't expect her freaking out and then calling to hang up on me to affect me the way that it does. I am not expecting the hurt I feel. To feel sad and empty. It's most likely the reason I'm sitting in front of Rian, sipping whiskey.

I never drink.

How pathetic?

Getting their DNA was simple. Scarlett gave it willingly. Charla, I knew, would not, so I swabbed her mouth one night after fucking when she passed out. Yeah, I'm a dick. So what?

"You should apologize, chicks like it when a dude apologizes."

My eyes snap up to Rian. "Who said I did anything wrong and that a chick is involved?"

"I'm not stupid, boss, I saw the blonde you were with

the other day. The way your hand rested on her back. You never touch any women like that. You stood way too close."

He has a good eye.

"It's nothing."

"It's something if you are sitting here drinking. Just tell her you are sorry."

"It's not that simple." It's not. Charla just had her life turned upside down. I played a part in that destruction.

"Look, if she has feelings for you, she'll listen to what you have to say. Trust me." Rian winks before moving down the bar, wiping it with a rag as he goes.

Maybe he's right.

———

I knock twice and wait. I don't know why I'm nervous, but I am. My palm is sweating, holding a bouquet of lilies. I hope she likes fucking flowers. Rich girls should anyway.

Spencer opens the door, his eyes narrowing on the flowers. "She's in the room." He moves back allowing me in. Truth be told, I wasn't expecting him to. I came ready to fight.

Knocking on her door, I stand back, holding my breath. When I don't get a response, I knock again.

"She probably won't answer," Spencer tells me as he walks down the hall.

I hate invading Charla's space, but I'm not leaving without talking to her. She'll at least me out before she decides to kick me out.

Turning the knob slowly, I peek in. The lights are dim and she's laying on the bed facing the windows that are open to the beach.

"Charla."

I watch as her entire body tenses. It makes me feel like pure shit. Of all the times we've been together, all the times I warned her I was no good for her, she never once seemed scared of me. Now, though, the way she stiffens. It's like taking a knife to the chest.

She doesn't reply, so I step in a little closer. I'm not good with this type of shit. Where do I even begin?

"I brought you flowers."

"That's nice, there's a trashcan in the bathroom."

Another jab to my chest. Fuck.

"Charla, let me explain."

"I don't want to hear it."

"Too bad." I hear her huff as I step in closer, closing the door behind me. I still don't care for Spencer. Even if we've come to an understanding for the time being.

"I should have told you first. I'm sorry I didn't."

"How long have you kept it from me?"

"A short while."

"While you were fucking me did you know?"

I swallow slowly. "I only recently got the results, but yes, we've fucked since I've gotten them."

"Why... why would you keep that from me?"

"I had to get back at your father. I wanted him to know how it felt to disrupt someone's life. You must understand that. I didn't do it to intentionally hurt you."

Charla sits up and doesn't look at me. She stares out at the water. "You did hurt me. The fact that you knew and you didn't tell me yourself. Then you went to the damn reporters. How could you?"

Her voice breaks with that question. It makes me feel things I'm not used to feeling. Walking up, I place the flowers on the bed and kneel down in front of her.

"I had to teach your father a lesson. That he doesn't get

to control all the cards. He let my mother out early because he couldn't control you. You see how fucked up that is, right? How he had such connections to make that happen?"

She has to see that. That her father fucked up too. More so than me.

"He was wrong, doing what he did to get back at you. I won't defend his shit actions, but I trusted you, East. I trusted you with everything I had in me, and you took that trust and broke it into a million pieces."

Charla stands from the bed and walks to the windows. I worry she'll do something stupid like jump. In a split second, I'm next to her.

"I'm sorry."

"I have a fucking twin sister and she works for you!" Charla turns and shoves me.

Hell, it's not like I knew this when Scarlett started working for me. Fuck. I put my arms up in surrender. I didn't even know they were twins until the results came back. I mean they have similarities. There's no denying. Both have blonde hair, Charla's is more vibrant. Their eyes, now those are almost identical. Their noses are a little different, Charla has higher cheekbones. It's what triggered me to do the DNA shit in the first place. When Scarlett said her birth father might have been wealthy, I started to put pieces together and knew what I needed to do.

"It's not like I knew this prior to her working for me. Fuck. You two lived very different lives. But that's not my fault. That's on your father."

For a second, I think she's going to slap me. Instead, she sags her shoulders and shakes her head.

"Tell me what I have to do to make this right?"

Where that came from, I don't know. I'm not one to fucking beg, yet here I am.

"Has she had a good life, my sister?"

I take a deep breath. This is one thing I will not lie to Charla about. No more lies. "No. Her mother, well, your mother too, forced her into stripping at the age of sixteen."

Charla glares at me and raises her hand. Backing up, I throw my hands up in defense. "Woah, that was before I was the owner."

"Unbelievable," she mutters, lowering her hand to stare back out to the ocean.

"Your mother was a stripper. It is how your father met her. He came in weekly, and she was the pretty one he always requested. I only know this because my grandfather told me Scarlett's story when I took over. I guess there was a slip-up and Rochelle got pregnant. There was paperwork and they came to an agreement that each got one twin."

"How could a mother do such a thing?"

"When you have an alcohol addiction, you do stupid things. Your mother was and still is an alcoholic. It's what forced Scarlett in. She was out of her prime, age and years of drinking ruined her. She threw her daughter in to pay the bills and that's where we are at today."

Charla covers her mouth as a sob escapes her. I reach out and pull her into me. I can tell she wants to resist me, yet she gives in easily as I wrap my arms around her waist. She cries into my shoulder, and I just hold her. There's nothing else I can do.

After a while the sobs quiet and she eventually pulls back to look at me.

"I want to meet my sister."

"Just say when, I'll make it happen."

Charla nods, looking out at the ocean.

"I'm so sorry," I say as I wipe a loose strand of golden hair from her face.

"I'm still mad at you, just so you know."

I love it when she's feisty. It makes things between us more entertaining.

"Be mad as long as you want."

Grabbing her chin, I turn her to look back at me, I wink. "You have a right to be mad. But just know, I'm still going to kiss you."

And that's exactly what I do.

46

CHARLA

Today I'm going to meet my sister. My twin sister to be exact. Scarlett. I'm not exactly sure how I feel about it yet. Will she hate me for getting to live a better life than her? Do I tell her I'm sorry she lived a shit life? So many thoughts cloud my mind right now. I can't focus.

Spencer chooses right then to walk in. I look up at my best friend. My best friend that has apparently been seeing my twin sister. Of course, he had no idea at first either, but I guess according to him, our eyes look the same. That's the reason he kept staring at me strangely. It makes sense now, though at the time it was creeping me out.

"Come on, it's time to go to lunch and meet Scarlett."

Smiling, I nod and turn down my computer. The one thing to get me through these past few weeks has been working. Plugging away and working on accounts kept me distracted.

I wasn't ready to meet my sister and now that it is happening, I'm anxious. Spencer has reassured me countless times that everything will be fine and that she is just as nervous as I am. East will be there too, so that adds to my nerves.

I've avoided him. I told him I needed space to process everything and to clear my head. He's been respectful. I'm not sure where East and I stand, if we stand anywhere. The last time we were together, he was different. Almost as if he cared. And when he kissed me, well, it was mind-blowing. He took his time and let's just say it made me weak. I wanted to strip right then and let him have his way. He didn't. At the time I wish he had, was even mad that he didn't. Looking back now, I know why he didn't. He wanted to prove to me that he could be worthy of more than just a fuck.

Spencer puts his arm around me as we make our way to the elevator. "All will be fine, Char. Trust me."

"That's easy for you to say. You don't have a missing twin out there."

"You never know, I could."

I shoot him a glance and he just laughs at me while walking into the elevator. It's going to be a long walk to lunch.

We make it to Leo's earlier than I expected. It's a posh restaurant centered in the downtown area. I figured with it being lunchtime, the commute would have taken longer.

I let Spencer do the talking to the hostess. I suddenly feel very insecure. I keep my head cast down, too afraid to look around and spot her.

A strong hand grips my chin roughly. Familiar dark eyes find mine.

"Don't do that."

"Don't do what?" I whisper, craving to hear more of his sexy voice. The same voice that has been haunting my dreams.

"Don't look down. You hold your head high. Understand?"

I nod. How can he say so little and yet it mean so much?

"Your sister is waiting, let's go."

I allow him to pull me along through the restaurant to a back corner. No one else is seated back here and I can't help but wonder if East, or maybe Spencer, requested that it be that way. Knowing how they both are, they probably paid to reserve this section just to be certain we would have some privacy.

As we approach the table, I see her, she's looking down at the menu, blonde hair hiding her face. My heart is pounding faster than it ever has before. I'm so nervous I think I might be sick.

"Scarlett," East says her name quietly as if he's afraid to scare her.

She turns and stands immediately, "Sir."

What?

East shakes his head. "We've been over this. East, call me East."

She pulls her bottom lip in between her teeth nodding. She's just as nervous.

"Charla, this is Scarlett. Scarlett, Charla."

East and Spencer step back, giving us a moment. We look each other up and down. She's dressed in jeans and a plain white t-shirt. Nothing fancy. Her face is void of any makeup. I, on the other hand, am wearing a grey pantsuit with black stilettos. My hair is curled and I have a little makeup on. It's clear how much we do look alike. It's also clear how different our worlds are and that makes my heart break.

"Hi," she says nervously.

I smile. "Hey." I'm unsure of what to do. There are so

many scenarios that I imagined in my head, but now that we are standing face to face, I come up empty.

We stare at each other a moment longer, silently assessing.

"I won't bite, come sit down."

Her words make me smile. I think I like her already. I pull up a chair and sit next to her.

She goes to hug me and pauses. "Is this okay?"

I nod and open my arms. She smells like strawberries, I think. This is okay. Everything will be okay. I look around but don't see the guys anywhere. They must be giving us space.

Pulling back, I smile. "I suppose we should get to know one another."

"Yes, I think we should. You go first. I want to hear all about how fucked up our father is and then I'll tell you about our screwed-up mother."

I laugh, a genuine laugh. "Deal."

47

CHARLA

It's been a month since Scarlett and I met. We like a lot of the same things. Our favorite color is yellow. We both love coffee. Our taste in music and food isn't quite the same, but when you grow up in very different homes, I guess that's to be expected.

We've had dinner every night since we met. She comes over or we go out. It's mostly going out. She's taken me by her place once and I cried sitting in the parking lot. It's not fair that she had to live and struggle while I was a spoiled rich girl. I'm grateful, though, that she doesn't hold it against me. Not at all. I have not and don't think I want to meet our mother, Rochelle. I've actually been trying to convince Scarlett to move in with me. She's not sure about leaving Rochelle behind though. It's something she is struggling with and has for a very long time. I refuse to let her strip. I demanded that she learn to bartend and still be paid a decent amount. East agreed. Of course, her dating Spencer might have something to do with that change in position, but I'll never ask.

Tonight, however, instead of dinner with Scarlett, I

have a date. An actual date with East Sinclair, that bad boy with a lip ring who once claimed he was wrong for me.

A knock sounds at my door. He's always on time. When I open the door, it's as if the devil himself is standing there. He's dressed in all black with the top buttons of his shirt left undone. His sleeves are rolled up, exposing his tattoos. His dark hair is styled just the way I like. When my eyes find his, he smirks.

"Ready for our date?"

"I am. And where will we be going on said date?"

"You'll see. Come on. Time is ticking."

I can't help but laugh. It's just like him and I should expect nothing different.

Burns is our driver. He's got the limo tonight, which strikes me as odd, but I don't question it. However, the minute we make a turn to head out of the city, I know instantly where we are going.

"We're going to your house?"

"Will it be a problem if we are?"

"No, but if you think our date is going to consist of you bringing me back to your house just to fuck me, I'd say that's hardly a date," I half joke.

I haven't slept with East since everything went down. He's tried and believe me, I wanted to give in many times. There's something about his touch that burns my body, and all coherent thoughts turn to ash. But no. I have stood my ground. I needed to be sure about him. About us. That he could do a real relationship. What does that even look like to a man like East? He's been different and while I am enjoying getting to know this version of him, I do miss how dark and rough he is. I miss how alive he makes my body feel. Which might be why I have a little surprise for him later.

"It most certainly is a date, Charla, and mark my words, after our date, I will be fucking you."

See, even his words ignite something inside of me to the point I have to squeeze my thighs.

East leans over, runs one finger up my thigh, under my denim skirt.

"I bet your pussy is soaked right now. Tell me, are you wet just thinking about what I just said?"

I'm unable to form any words as my breathing kicks it up a notch. He continues dragging his finger up. When he reaches the apex of my thighs and realizes I'm not wearing anything under my skirt, his eyes shoot to mine. Black eyes full of desire stare back.

"Charla, Charla, Charla," he says as he dips a finger in to find me wet, just like he said I would be.

"East." My voice trembles as he continues to slowly pump his finger.

"It looks like you brought me an appetizer, one I'll gladly snack on."

In one swift move, he grabs my thighs pulling me into a laying position against the leather seat. He kneels down and shoves my skirt up above my ass. The anticipation of what's to come is killing me. I've made us both wait long enough.

And the minute his tongue glides along my slit, all thoughts of dinner go out the window. I'm no longer hungry for food. The only hunger I have is that of East Sinclair and he can feast on me for the rest of the night.

THE END

ACKNOWLEDGMENTS

Readers - Thank you for reading Shattered Illusion. Thank you for reading and supporting indie authors. We couldn't do what we do without you.

To my beta babes- Thank you for reading early copies and giving me your input to help make Charla and East's story perfect.

To my arc babes- Thank you reading and reviewing. Your endless support means so much to me.

To my street team babes- Thank you for helping share all things Shattered Illusion. You all rock!

Book Bloggers- Thank you for your love of reading and sharing all things bookish.

To my editor, Beth- You are damn amazing. That is all.

To my cover designer, Amanda- When I saw your pre-made, Charla's story immediately came to me. I had to have it. Your design skills are amazing and the reason Shattered Illusion exists, so thank you.

To my husband- Thanks for always being my number one fan. For always encouraging me to keep going when I feel like I'm failing.

To my children, especially my teenager- Please stop telling your friends what I write. There's a reason my books are labeled 18+. The rest of you, don't do what your older sibling is doing. Oh, and I love you.

PLAYLIST

We Don't Have to Dance - Andy Black
Champagne & Sunshine - PLVTINUM & Tarro
Why Are You Here - Machine Gun Kelly
Dizzy - MISSIO
The Liars Club - Coheed & Cambria
Angel With A Shotgun - The Cab
Empty - PVRIS

Want more of The Red Society?
Sign up for Lisamarie Kade's newsletter to stay in touch on
book two: Scarlett and Spencer's story.

Lisamarie Kade's newsletter sign up

ABOUT THE AUTHOR

Lisamarie Kade is a romance author living in the sunshine state with her husband and small army of children.

When not writing, she can be found chasing the kids around or volunteering for one of their many activities.

Lisamarie enjoys chocolate peanut butter cups, music, and reading something steamy while sipping sweet wine.

facebook.com/lisamariekadeauthor

amazon.com/author/lisamariekade

tiktok.com/@lisamariekadeauthor?

bookbub.com/profile/lisamarie-kade

pinterest.com/lisamariekadeauthor

ALSO BY LISAMARIE KADE

The Secrets We Keep

Mended Hearts

The War Within

The Christmas Breakdown